FESTIVAL FEVER

Fleur Denman is given the chance of a lifetime to front the Ridgly Parva Arts and History Festival — but some locals have long memories, and aren't prepared to overlook the scandal that once blackened the Denman name. In the face of adversity, Fleur sets out to prove her worth. Then some festival money goes missing, and Ben Salt, the main sponsor, is among the first to point an accusing finger in her direction. To make matters worse, Fleur finds herself increasingly attracted to him . . .

Books by Margaret Mounsdon
in the Linford Romance Library:

THE MIMOSA SUMMER
THE ITALIAN LAKE
LONG SHADOWS
FOLLOW YOUR HEART
AN ACT OF LOVE
HOLD ME CLOSE
A MATTER OF PRIDE
SONG OF MY HEART
MEMORIES OF LOVE
WRITTEN IN THE STARS
MY SECRET LOVE
A CHANCE ENCOUNTER
SECOND TIME AROUND
THE HEART OF THE MATTER
LOVE TRIUMPHANT
NIGHT MUSIC
FIT FOR LOVE
THE POWER OF LOVE
THE SWALLOW HOUSE SUMMER
ANGELA'S RETURN HOME
LOVE AMONG THE ARTS
FINN'S FOREST
LOVE IN A MIST

MARGARET MOUNSDON

FESTIVAL FEVER

Complete and Unabridged

ST. HELENS
COMMUNITY
LIBRARIES

ACC. No.

CLASS No.

LINFORD
Leicester

First published in Great Britain in 2016

First Linford Edition
published 2017

Copyright © 2016 by Margaret Mounsdon
All rights reserved

A catalogue record for this book is available
from the British Library.

ISBN 978–1–4448–3222–8

Published by
F. A. Thorpe (Publishing)
Anstey, Leicestershire

Set by Words & Graphics Ltd.
Anstey, Leicestershire
Printed and bound in Great Britain by
T. J. International Ltd., Padstow, Cornwall

This book is printed on acid-free paper

1

Fleur was dreading her forthcoming interview.

'It goes with the job,' Yvette insisted. 'Now are you interested?'

Fleur didn't have a choice. The family scandal had been years ago, but people had long memories, and offers for her services were not thick on the ground.

'Thanks, Yvette. You're a star.'

'I'll take that as a yes then, shall I?' Yvette nodded. 'Be prepared for anything,' she warned.

Fleur's feet sank into the mud of Brampton's Field. Yvette had networked tirelessly to gain the prime slot on the lunchtime chat show. They had been given a fantastic chance to promote the first Ridgly Parva Arts and History Festival, and as chief liaison officer Fleur was desperate not to let Yvette down.

A legion of Roman soldiers marched

past, breastplates gleaming in the sunshine, their breath misting the morning air. Although it was May, Ridgly Parva was still suffering unseasonably chilly weather. Fleur saluted the soldiers before diving into the back of a lighting engineers' van. Negotiating her way round wire cables and socket sets, she changed out of her mud-stained outfit into a smarter pair of jeans and emerged looking marginally smarter and ready for the local media.

Fleur glanced around the field. Their host, the notoriously reclusive Ben Salt, had yet to put in an appearance. His agent had proved as difficult to get hold of as the great man himself. Her calls had gone unanswered and she hadn't received so much as a publicity photo.

'Don't worry, darling, I'm sure I'll recognise him,' her mother, Phyllis, had reassured her over their hurried breakfast.

'I don't see how if we don't know what he looks like,' Fleur pointed out.

'I'll man the main gate. He won't get past me. When he arrives I'll introduce myself, then escort him over to you.'

'I hope he doesn't sneak in the back way.' Fleur swallowed the last of her toast. She didn't share her mother's confidence. Ben Salt sounded like the sort of man who broke rules.

'What have I taught you about positive thinking?' Phyllis raised a plucked eyebrow.

Fleur gave her a shamefaced smile. Her mother had been a tower of strength when their life had collapsed around them. 'Sorry, I won't let you down.' She kissed Phyllis's cheek. 'Go get 'em.'

'Where do you pick up these expressions?' Phyllis shuddered.

The clang of metal on scaffolding echoed around the field, and a loud explosion from the combat arena followed by a puff of smoke rattled the poles against the sturdy supporting framework. A group of excited children brandishing homemade swords raced past Fleur, who stepped backwards, anxious to avoid being flattened by the junior branch of the Ridgly Parva

Civil War re-enactment group.

The Battle of Ridgly Parva was well-documented in the local archives. It had taken place in this very field when the fiercely royalist inhabitants of Ridgly Parva had fought the Parva Minor round-heads from sunrise to sunset until both sides collapsed, too exhausted to continue, and an honourable draw was announced.

'Sorry,' a harassed teacher mouthed at Fleur from the rear of her little troop. She was clutching a selection of tabards and helmets and doing her best to keep up with her charges as they disappeared in the direction of the living-history village. Like Fleur, her feet were sinking into the mud, the consequence of a week of relentless rain. The sun was making a brave attempt to break through the grey clouds but so far without much success.

Mentally rehearsing the power points of her interview, Fleur didn't hear mo-torbike revs approaching from the rear.

'Look out,' a voice shouted.

Fleur turned. Her feet sank into the soft earth and stayed there. She was trapped and on a collision course with the biggest motorbike she had ever seen in her life. The rider swerved. Mud flew through the air. A ball of warm, sticky brown slime hit her ear and trickled down her neck.

'What the —?' she shrieked.

The leather-clad biker performed another semicircle, then slid to a halt. He killed his engine, removed his helmet, and ran a hand through his hair.

'Whoops.' He spoke with a mild transatlantic twang. 'I didn't mean that to happen.'

Fleur's temperament matched her red hair. 'You oaf!' she bellowed. 'Look what you've done.'

'You weren't paying attention to where you were going,' he retaliated.

'I'm entitled to walk on the grass.'

The man's arrogance was beyond belief. A crooked smile tugged at the corner of his mouth. 'You do have a point,' he acknowledged.

Fleur steeled her resolve. She'd always had a thing for men with brown eyes, but this was neither the time nor the place. 'I've got more than a point,' she said. 'I've got right on my side.'

'Sorry I sprayed you.' His voice betrayed no evidence of regret. 'But it's really not sensible to wear white jeans in a muddy field.'

'Neither is driving like a maniac in a restricted area.' Fleur finally freed her feet from the mud.

'Mind that tent peg,' he cautioned as she regained her balance.

The public address system stuttered into life. 'Fleur Denman to the media tent immediately, please. Fleur Denman.'

Fleur crossed her arms in confrontation. 'What do you suggest I do now?' She smiled through gritted teeth. 'I'm due on air.'

'You're Fleur Denman?'

'I am.'

The man scratched the back of his head. 'You do have a bit of a problem, don't you?' he agreed.

'So do you. Only authorised vehicles are allowed on site.'

'What constitutes an authorised vehicle?'

'Certainly not bikes like that monster.' The silver logo glinted back at Fleur.

'But a Sherman tank's OK?'

An armoured personnel carrier trundled past.

'How's it going, gang?' the biker greeted the youngsters escorting it across the field.

'Brilliant,' they chorused.

'Catch up with you later.' He turned his attention back to Fleur. 'Where were we?'

'You'd just plastered me with mud and I was calling you the most inconsiderate, mule-headed ...' She paused to get her breath.

'Yes, I get the picture. If you'd like to grab a shower,' he stalled her tirade, 'I'll cover for you.'

'I can't appear in front of the cameras looking like some sort of swamp monster.'

'Shower first?'

'We don't run to such on-site luxuries.'

'Tricky situation.' His face creased in concern.

An interested group of spectators had begun to gather around them. One or two of them pointed at Fleur and giggled.

'Where's your pass?' Fleur peered at the man's leather jacket.

'Do I need one?'

She was struck by a sudden thought. 'Are you an activist?'

'A what?'

'Have you come here to stir up trouble?'

'Why would I want to do that?'

'Some of the villagers are against the festival. They've been forming protest groups and holding demonstrations on the green.'

'Not me. I'm all for it.'

Yvette Palmer strode towards them. 'Can you keep the noise down? We're trying to conduct an interview in the press tent. Fleur, you're on next.' She did a double take. 'Heavens, what have you been doing? Mud-wrestling a hippo?'

'Get hold of security and have this person evicted.'

A perplexed frown wrinkled Yvette's

forehead. 'What? Why?'

'He's a danger to the public.'

'No I'm not,' the man contradicted.

'That machine of his is a menace.'

'It's not a machine,' he protested, 'it's an Italian legend.'

'I don't care what it is. Get it off site now.' Fleur clenched her teeth.

Yvette raised a hand. 'Hold on, Fleur.'

The public address system made another impassioned plea for Fleur's immediate presence in the press tent.

'Could I help explain things to the publicity team?' the man intervened.

'You've done more than enough.' Fleur had great difficulty keeping the scorn out of her voice.

'I got held up on the motorway,' he explained to Yvette.

'Then don't let us hold you up any further. The exit's that way.' Fleur was making ineffectual attempts to brush mud off her sweater.

'A female at the gate wearing a huge hat wouldn't let me in. She said as I didn't have a pass, I was going to have to go the long way round.'

Fleur edged her way back into the exchange. 'It's a pity you didn't take her advice. And before you say anything you might later regret, the lady you are referring to is the mayor, who also happens to be my mother.'

'I thought I saw a resemblance.' His smile still tugged the corner of his mouth.

'No you didn't,' Fleur contradicted him.

'Maybe not,' he agreed. 'Your mother's an elegant lady.'

Fleur was now struggling to catch her breath. It had been a long time since she had lost her cool, but this man was pressing all the wrong buttons.

'Anyway,' he continued his explanation, 'I couldn't hang about for a pass. I was pressed for time, so I made my apologies and drove round her.'

'Do you ride roughshod over everyone?' Fleur demanded.

'What was I supposed to do? This was an emergency.'

A breathy power-suited female wobbled

towards them on impossibly high heels. 'Hey, guys,' she shouted, gesturing to her back-up crew, 'I've got a great idea. Bring the cameras over here. Let's do the interview al fresco.'

Fleur watched in disbelief as canvas chairs were hurriedly produced and mobile cameras wheeled onto the grass. Within moments the crowd around them had grown significantly, and a makeshift studio had been set up before the familiar theme tune of the lunchtime chat show spilled out of the loudspeakers.

'What a fantastic angle we can give this one.' Cassie de Vere was bustling around issuing clipboards and instructions to her underlings. 'Fleur, isn't it? You'd better sit on a towel. Don't want you messing up company property, do we? Did you come off worse after a disagreement with an Anglo-Saxon?' she sniggered.

The bike rider raised a hand. 'Guilty. I sprayed Ms Denman.'

'I'm sure it wasn't your fault,' Cassie

cooed.

'Yvette,' Fleur hissed, 'do something.'

'I'm thinking on my feet.'Yvette ducked to avoid colliding with an overhead microphone. 'There must be a way we can turn this disaster to our advantage.'

'I can't appear on air like this.'

'You're going to have to. Improvise. Make light of it. I mean, what's a bit of mud?'

'What's that make-up girl doing?' Fleur demanded.

'Her job, I'd say,'Yvette replied with a wry twist of her lips as Fleur watched the new arrival having his hair styled.

'But she's ...' Before Fleur could finish her sentence, the truth dawned on her. 'That's Ben Salt, isn't it?'

'I tried to tell you,'Yvette insisted.

'Silence please,' a technician called, waving his arms. 'Everybody ready?'The lunchtime theme tune swung into action. 'Over to you, Cassie.'

Fleur looked into the amused face of the owner of Castle Brampton as the cameras began to roll.

2

'That was fantastic,' Cassie gushed. 'I wish all our guests were so easy to interview.' She batted her false eyelashes at Ben.

'Thank you,' he replied with a polite nod. 'Now, if you'll excuse me …'

'Of course. You must have masses of things to do. Maybe we'll see you around later?' Cassie asked hopefully.

'Maybe,' he agreed, before easing his lean frame out of the canvas chair. He stretched his legs and strolled away from the makeshift studio.

Phyllis Denman, who had been waiting in the wings, pounced. 'I want a word with you, young man.'

'Hello again.' Ben smiled. 'What can I do for you? I understand you're the mayor.'

'There's something we need to sort out.'

'And that is?'

Fleur raced across the grass and grabbed her mother's elbow. 'Mum —'

'Please, Fleur, leave this to me.' Phyllis gently removed her daughter's hand and again addressed Ben. 'You had no right to drive past me in such an aggressive manner.'

'I've already had the lecture.' Ben's smile was wearing thin.

'I managed to move out of your way, but I see my daughter wasn't so lucky. What have you got to say for yourself?' Phyllis's grey eyes did not return Ben's smile.

Yvette glided between them. 'Phyllis, may I introduce you to Ben Salt?'

The flowers on Phyllis's hat were still trembling. 'And you could have told me who you were,' she added for good measure.

'You didn't give me much of a chance,' Ben explained, 'but I do apologise for all the trouble I've caused. I had no idea I had to have a security pass and that I wasn't allowed to ride a motorbike through my own field. It won't happen again. The public will be perfectly safe, and in future I'll follow the letter of the law. Promise.'

Phyllis acknowledged Ben's apology with a gracious inclination of her head. 'So you are the owner of Castle Brampton?' the slightly mollified woman asked in her best mayoral tones.

'I am,' he acknowledged, 'although to be honest I've always felt calling it a castle was a bit ambitious of old Sir Isaac Brampton, even if it has got a moat, a drawbridge, and a portcullis. It's more of a mini-castle, wouldn't you say? And the surrounding land is exactly the right place to hold an arts festival.'

A silence fell between them. Ben made an encouraging face at Fleur. 'If we're still talking to each other, I think it's your turn to say something,' he prompted.

Contrary to Fleur's expectations, the interview had gone well. Ben had accepted full blame for Fleur's dishevelled appearance and explained it was due to his late arrival on site and not to any lack of professionalism on Fleur's behalf. After that, Fleur had relaxed, and when the microphone had been turned in her direction she had been able to join in the jokes about mud swamps and the hazards of being chief liaison officer at events held in unreliable fields.

'A folly,' Fleur spoke up in reply to Ben's prompt.

'Come again?' He frowned at her.

'A mini-castle is called a folly,' Fleur repeated, remembering her history lessons at school.

'Brampton's Folly? I like the sound of that,' Ben agreed. 'But whatever you call it, it's where I enjoy my down time. A place where I kick off my shoes and chill.'

'As you know, Phyllis,' Yvette said, sounding determined to keep the exchange upbeat, 'Ben has generously donated the use of his grounds for the inaugural Ridgly Parva Arts and History Festival, and I know you'd like to join me in expressing our gratitude to him for his generosity.'

'Well, of course,' Phyllis agreed, adding

a belated, 'Thank you, Mr Salt.'

'Ben, please.'

'And I'm Mrs Denman. Phyllis.' They shook hands.

'We'll do our best to keep disruption to a minimum,' Yvette assured him, anxious to keep things on an even keel.

'I'm sure you will.' Ben smiled ruefully as there was yet another mini-explosion from the re-enactment area.

'Ben has also agreed to be our keynote speaker on Sunday afternoon — quite a coup, wouldn't you agree?' Yvette smiled at Phyllis and Fleur.

'Well, I don't know much about motorbikes,' Phyllis acknowledged, 'but I'm sure there'll be some here who'll find the subject of interest.'

'Ben won't be talking about motorbikes,' Yvette said with a trace of annoyance.

'He won't?' Phyllis looked surprised. 'What will you be talking about, then?'

'Rex Flint,' Fleur supplied the answer.

'Ben's written a string of novels,' Yvette explained.

'Featuring this Rex Flint?' Phyllis asked.

'That's right,' her daughter replied.

'All bestsellers,' Yvette added.

'Have you read any of them, Phyllis?'

'I'm afraid I don't have much time for reading. Fleur?' She looked to her daughter.

Before Fleur could reply, Ben asked, 'Are you amongst those who think my books are highly improbable nonsense?'

Fleur hesitated, reluctant to admit that she had stayed up late into the night to finish his latest novel. What made them so special was the character of Rex Flint, a hard-nosed private detective who had no issues about portraying the softer side of his nature. He regularly got things wrong and frequently fell foul of the authorities in all five continents. He experienced emotions with which his readers could identify, and they loved him all the more for his weaknesses.

Legions of fans would eagerly await Ben's newest novel, setting up chat rooms and online discussion groups to debate the plot line and to put forward theories as to what would be the latest development in Rex Flint's unpredictable life.

'I love Rex Flint,' Fleur was forced to admit.

'No kidding?' Ben looked inordinately pleased by her praise. 'Which book is your favourite?'

'*Don't Send Me Roses*,' Fleur replied, remembering how she had raced through the final chapters, narrowly missing her stop on the London Underground because she had been so engrossed in the story.

'Well, you may be this year's keynote speaker,' Phyllis said, moderating the tone of her voice, 'but at the risk of repeating myself, you really can't go riding around on that monster in the middle of a busy field, whether you own the field or not.'

'It won't happen again,' Ben promised. 'Or if it does, I'll make sure I've got the correct pass.'

Fleur flushed. Her mother didn't always realise when she was being teased, and if someone didn't stop her she would probably take Ben's comments seriously and start issuing him with instructions on how to obtain a high-visibility jacket.

'Phyllis?' a technician called over. 'We're ready for your interview.'

'Goodness.' Phyllis adjusted her hat. 'How do I look?' she asked.

'Stunning as always,' Fleur assured her mother.

'Try not to upset anyone else, will you, darling?' Phyllis looked over her daughter's shoulder to where Ben was polishing the chrome on his motorbike. 'We've a lot riding on the success of the festival. It's going to put Ridgly Parva on the literary map, you see.'

After a second prompt to hurry up, Phyllis bustled over to the media tent.

'Your mother's quite an act, isn't she?' Ben looked to where Phyllis was now busy charming the socks off a suited and booted businessman.

'She's unique,' Fleur agreed with an indulgent smile.

Since being voted in as mayor, Phyllis has thrown herself into her duties with a zeal that astounded her daughter. After her father's death, Fleur had worried that her mother wouldn't be able to cope with the challenges of everyday life. Her father had done absolutely everything for the family. Phyllis hadn't even needed to fill the car with petrol; and as for changing a blown fuse, the concept would have been beyond her. But when the opportunity arose for her to become mayor, she had shamelessly canvassed for votes, made speeches, and pulled out all the self-promotion stops. It was only Fleur who recognised the occasional crack in her mother's confident veneer, and on those occasions she did everything to support her.

'I hope she's not too mad at me,' Ben said.

'I expect she was annoyed that you managed to get past her,' Fleur admitted. 'You are part of a select group. There aren't many who've managed it.'

They shared a complicit smile.

'Ben, I've masses of paperwork for you to look at, and absolutely everyone wants a piece of you,' Yvette said, getting down to business. 'So if there's nothing further here, can we get on?'

'Fine by me,' Ben agreed. 'If you'd like to freshen up at the house, Fleur, feel free. The housekeeper is expecting me back, so there'll be loads of hot water and towels. Help yourself.'

'I think I'd better go home and change, if that's all right with you, Yvette?'

'Don't take too long about it, will you?'

'I'll be as quick as I can,' Fleur promised.

Ben squinted at Fleur's name badge. 'Denman?' He frowned. 'Are you any relation to Edwin Denman?'

'He was my father,' Fleur replied in a quiet voice. 'Now if you'll excuse me, I have a lot to attend to.' She strode off in the direction of the exit.

Abe Groves ambled out of the artisan craft and carpentry workshop. 'My, you've got a face on you,' he said, looking at Fleur.

'Abe,' she greeted him. As one of nature's gentlemen with never a bad word to say about anyone, he always cheered her up. 'It's been one of those days,' she admitted.

'Fancy a pick-me-up? I'm on my break.'

'I was on my way home to change.'

'I shouldn't bother. By the end of the day everyone on site is usually carrying his or her body weight in mud. You won't look any different from the rest of them.'

'Is that supposed to make me feel better?' Fleur asked.

'It's the best I can do by way of a compliment. Come on, I'll treat you to a piece of cake. Bet you didn't have any lunch, did you?'

'I forgot,' Fleur confessed.

'In that case,' Abe insisted, 'we're having the works. The tea tent is this way.'

'What makes you such a nice person?'

'It's the company I keep.' He grinned back at her. 'And you haven't asked me about my day.'

Fleur hastened to make amends for her lapse. 'Right. What did you do?'

'We made little wooden clogs, then

baskets for the garden, and a miniature wooden table and matching chairs. I answered questions until my brain hurt, then to my great relief a teacher arrived and we were all let out for the day.'

Seated opposite Abe, Fleur tucked into a plate of scones and drank two mugs of hot tea. Abe was comfortable company and didn't require a constant steam of chatter while they got down to the serious business of eating.

'Feel better?' he asked as he drained the teapot.

'Much,' Fleur admitted. 'You're even beginning to look handsome,' she teased. 'The light must be fading from the day.'

'You probably need glasses,' he retaliated. 'Are we on for tonight?'

'Tonight?'

'The barn dance. You'd forgotten, hadn't you?'

'I'm sorry, Abe. Yes, I had.'

'The Hayseeds are expecting you to make a guest appearance. Of course, if you've had a better offer …'

'I haven't.' All thoughts of having a

quiet night in vanished. Abe had been one of the people who had been there for Fleur when her world had fallen apart. Now she never let him down if she could help it. 'Are the others on form?'

'Raring to go. It'll be a blast.'

'I'll be there,' Fleur promised. 'Thanks for the tea, Abe. See you later. If I'm going to be on stage I really have to change.'

'Right-ho.' Abe stood up. 'Back to the workbench.'

On impulse, Fleur leaned forward and kissed him on the cheek.

'What was that for?' he asked in a gruff voice.

'Just for being you,' Fleur replied. 'Don't ever change.'

'I'll do my best,' he assured her.

As Fleur straightened up, she could feel eyes boring a hole in her back. Spinning round, she saw Ben Salt standing in the entrance to the tea tent.

3

'Ben,' Fleur greeted him. 'Do you know Abe Groves?'

'We've met.' Abe put out an eager hand.

Ben shook it in a distracted manner. 'We have?' he queried.

'A few weeks ago. You were on a deadline and The Hayseeds were rehearsing in the barn. We'd no idea you were at home or that we were disturbing you. We can get a bit loud on occasion. We'd let rip because we thought we had the place to ourselves.'

'Right, yes. Good to see you again.' All the time Ben was talking, he was staring at Fleur. 'And you didn't disturb me,' he added. 'I'd finished up for the day. I was written out, so I came to see what was going on.'

'That was a great evening, wasn't it?' Abe enthused.

'One of the best,' Ben agreed.

'Ben stayed on,' Abe explained to Fleur, 'then a party sort of developed.' Abe looked from him and back to Fleur, his cheerful smile never faltering. 'I'd best be getting on. I've a mountain of clearing up to do. You would not believe the mess some youngsters make. I've got wood shavings all over the place. Eight o'clock sharp tonight, Fleur. If you feel like another party, Ben, join us.'

'There's a barn dance in the offing,' Fleur explained.

'I can't promise anything,' Ben replied.

'And I can't say I blame you for chickening out. My singing isn't all it's cracked up to be,' Fleur said.

'You sing?' Ben sounded surprised.

'My voice isn't up to much, but Abe's a difficult man to refuse.' Fleur's attempts to get Ben to lighten up were meeting with little success. 'Is there anything I can do for you?' she asked when he didn't respond.

'I came to tell you my kitchen floor's flooded.'

'What?' Fleur frowned.

'There's water all over the place.'

'Is there?'

'Are you responsible?'

'Of course I'm not,' Fleur protested indignantly, her fragile good will towards Ben Salt evaporating in an instant.

'Mrs Philpott says she left a large notice on the front and it's not there now.'

'What's not there now? And on the front of what?' Fleur was growing exceedingly confused.

'The washing machine. It's out of order.' Ben spoke patiently, as if addressing a child.

'Then may I suggest you get it mended? In case you haven't noticed, I'm still covered in mud, so you're going to have to look elsewhere for the culprit — but please don't start slinging any more wild accusations at innocent individuals. I think I can speak for most of the team, and none of them would dream of using your washing machine without your permission. I don't even think any of them have actually been inside your castle or folly or whatever it's called. We're polite in Ridgly Parva. We tend to wait for invitations first.'

'I seem to recall extending an invitation for you to freshen up inside.'

'Do you also recall me telling Yvette that I was going home to change?'

'Then why didn't you?'

'If it's any of your business, I bumped into Abe. We had tea together.'

'Very cosy.'

Fleur clenched her fists. Her family had been on the receiving end of more than their fair share of natural injustice over the years, and she'd long ago decided not to suffer any more. 'If you weren't so important to the festival, I'd be sorely tempted to tell you what you can do with your flooded floor,' she responded.

Ben's smile transformed his face. 'I suppose I asked for that,' he acknowledged.

'It's because my name's Denman, isn't it?'

Fleur had grown up the hard way after her father's fall from grace. When her mother had managed to pick up the pieces of their shattered family name, Fleur had decided her only choice was to follow Phyllis's dignified example.

'You think I can't be trusted,' he said.

'Hello, folks.' A gangly individual wearing a battered straw hat, jeans, and an ill-fitting linen jacket ambled over. He fixed his magnetic blue eyes on Fleur. 'Are you getting in training for the Civil War re-enactment?' he asked before embracing her.

'Sandy,' Ben said, sounding annoyed, 'you told me you were arriving tomorrow.'

'Did I?' he asked vaguely.

Fleur drew away from Sandy in dismay. 'Your jacket — it's covered in mud streaks.'

'Never mind. It'll come out in the wash.' He raised his straw hat. 'Fleur,' he said, reading her name badge. 'You must be the lovely lady who's been leaving numerous messages for me. I'm sorry I didn't get back to you, but I'm hopeless with technology. Ask anyone.'

'Sandy calls himself my agent.' Ben still sounded annoyed.

Fleur gaped at Ben's elusive agent. 'You're Alexander Ambrose?'

'Known to one and all as Sandy.'

The expression on Ben's face matched Fleur's exasperated look. 'I know, I know — an agent who doesn't do technology. It doesn't get much worse than that, does it?'

'Talking of technology,' Sandy confided with a guilty grimace, 'I've a confession to make, Ben.'

'Oh yes?' There was a wary note in Ben's voice.

'Please don't go ballistic.'

'What have you done now?' Ben asked with a patient sigh.

'When I arrived I was rather travel-weary, so I nipped up to yours to grab a change of clothes.'

'I thought that jacket looked familiar. It's the one I wear when I'm gardening,' Ben observed.

'Is it? Anyway, to cut a long story short, I've messed up the washing machine.'

'It was you?' Ben now looked ready to explode.

'However, all is not lost,' Sandy hastened to reassure him. 'The lovely Yvette says there's a friendly plumber on site who she's sure will be more than willing to fix things. I'm off to find him now. I've been told he and his family are bashing out herbs in the Medieval Medicine Market. Think I'll join them. If I'm not there, you'll find me in the mead tent later. I need to stimulate my creative juices. So if anyone cares for a communal sip ...'

Sandy exited the tent and tagged onto a re-enactment detachment. Soon everyone was laughing at his antics as he entered the spirit of the roleplay.

'I owe you an apology,' Ben said to Fleur.

'It seems you do,' she agreed.

'Sandy can be unreliable,' he tried to explain.

'So I see.'

'He takes off at a moment's notice to write poetry or to visit his vineyard in France. He holds wine seminars that can go on for days. By all accounts they're lively affairs. He actually knows a lot about the history of the wine industry.'

'How on earth did he come to be your agent?' Fleur asked.

'It's a long story. I suppose you couldn't eat a second tea?'

'I beg your pardon?'

'I can't remember when I last ate, and there's a rumour doing the rounds that the ladies on the cake stall are selling off their produce at half price. You're not on a diet or anything, are you?'

'I don't have time for things like that.'

'Glad to hear it. So are we on?' There was a hopeful note in Ben's voice. 'I'll pay to make up for being such a boor-headed oaf, or whatever it was you called me.'

'If you twist my arm, I'm very partial to Mrs Rathbone's double coffee cream sponge,' Fleur relented, hoping the waistband of her jeans would withstand the onslaught.

'I'll get the cake. You grab the tea. Meet you back here in five minutes.'

He vanished and reappeared shortly afterward, staggering towards Fleur while doing his best to cope under the weight of a tray overloaded with sandwiches and cakes.

'Are you going to eat all that?' Fleur asked.

'I was hoping you'd help me out.' Ben settled down at the wobbly wooden table and began sorting out his purchases. 'Your Mrs Rathbone is a super-efficient salesperson. She talked me into buying the last of her rock cakes, a fruit bun, several cheese and pickle sandwiches, and the biggest double coffee cream sponge I have ever seen in my life. Tuck in.'

'The same goes for the ladies in the tea tent. We got the last contents of the urn, so it might be a bit stewed.'

'As long as it's brown and warm, that'll do me.' He took a healthy bite out of a sandwich and chewed. Like Abe, he didn't seem to see the need to talk while eating.

Fleur cut a hefty wedge of coffee cake and, intending only to nibble at the icing, found to her surprise she managed to eat it all.

'It must be the fresh air giving me an appetite,' she insisted as she also managed to polish off the last cheese and pickle sandwich and half a fruit bun.

'Summer festivals always do this,' Ben agreed.

'Have you been to many?'

'This is the first one I've hosted,' he admitted. 'Sandy talked me into it. Can you keep a secret?'

'Try me.'

'He's taken a shine to Yvette.'

Fleur spluttered into her tea. Ben thumped her on the back.

'Better?' he asked when Fleur had finished coughing.

'Did I hear you right?' She dabbed at her streaming eyes with a tissue.

'Yvette was scouting around for a suitable location for the festival and somehow she and Sandy linked up. I tell you, he's smitten.'

'She never mentioned anything to me.'

'I don't think she knows about it. Poor old Sandy, he's shy when it comes to this sort of thing. Anyway, in an effort to impress Yvette he put Brampton's Field forward as a possible location. Before I could stop him, I'd also been volunteered as a speaker.'

'It's not your sort of thing, is it?' Fleur sympathised, remembering his aversion to self-publicity.

'It's too late to cancel now.' Ben grinned. 'Seriously, though, it's fine. The field needs to be used, and if it's helping the community then so much the better.' He ducked as a paper missile narrowly avoided clipping the tip of his ear. 'What was that?'

'Sorry,' a breathless youngster panted, rushing towards them. 'I'm on aviation skills.'

'Remind me never to fly on one of your aircraft.' Ben handed back the crumpled missile. 'Would you and your friends like to finish these off?' He thrust some uneaten rock cakes into his hands.

'Wicked.'

'Where did you and Sandy meet?' Fleur asked after the boy had delivered a toothy smile and raced off.

'At school. He was the dreamy artistic one and I was the daredevil. One day we wound up in the sick bay together. I'd fallen off a fence, and Sandy was reading a book and hadn't been looking where he was going. He walked into a wall. They say opposites attract, and we got on like a house on fire. When I got a weekend job hefting market vegetables about the place, Sandy tagged along, and he's been doing it ever since.'

'I like him,' Fleur admitted.

'So do I.' Ben made a face. 'That's my problem. Flooding the kitchen is the latest in a long line of disasters. He's always sorry afterwards, and to give him credit he usually manages to sort everything out. Life would be dull without him. I appointed him as my agent because there's no one I'd trust more. He has his faults, but he's loyal, and in this world that counts for everything.'

'I can't see Sandy structuring book deals.' Fleur frowned.

'He doesn't, really. He does all the soft stuff — the fetching and carrying, sorting out the daily trivia. I would be lost without him, but when it comes to the business side of things I'm hands-on.'

'And Rex Flint?'

'What about him?'

'Is he you?'

'I'm always being asked that question, and the answer is no. I invented him one day when I was hospitalised.' Ben held up a hand. 'That's all I'm prepared to say.'

Sandy re-appeared and grabbed up a cheese sandwich that had escaped everyone's attention. 'He fell off his bike,' he said, 'showing off as usual. Just to update you on the kitchen situation, Ben, our friendly plumber is on his way now to deal with the problem.' He frowned at the table. 'Is that tea? It looks more like mud.'

'Don't mention mud, if you please.' Ben frowned at Sandy.

'I've learned something interesting about our Fleur.'

Fleur felt her face flame. 'What?' she demanded, hoping it wasn't going to be a rerun of her family's scandal-hit past.

'When she was living in a hostel, the girls complained about her.'

'Why?' Ben asked.

'They couldn't get to sleep. She used to read your books by torchlight under the bedclothes. It got so bad she was in danger of being chucked out.'

'How did you find out?' Fleur demanded.

'I've been talking to Yvette.' Sandy looked very pleased with himself. 'She's agreed to go to the barn dance with me tonight.'

'Now's your chance to get even, Fleur,' Ben confided. 'I can tell you things about Sandy.'

'You wouldn't.' Sandy sounded alarmed.

'Try me.'

'Do your worst,' Sandy said with a look of resignation.

'When it comes to dancing, Sandy's got two left feet.'

It was now Sandy's turn to get into his stride. 'If we're talking about blowing covers, I'll tell Fleur that when you were a stuntman you almost flattened a superstar because you were going too fast on that infernal machine of yours.'

'The brakes locked up.'

'As if.'

'I know how to ride my machine,' Ben insisted.

'Course you do,' Sandy agreed with an infuriating grin, 'as long as everyone stays out of your way. Wouldn't you agree, Fleur?'

Fleur opened her mouth to reply, but before she could a husky voice interrupted: 'Is this a private party or can anyone join in?'

Sandy groaned. Fleur turned round. A stabbing pain in her chest reminded her to breathe. Rebecca Ebony, the bestselling novelist, was standing inches away from her — only, when Fleur had been at school, Rebecca Ebony had been known as Becky the Bully.

4

'Rebecca,' Ben greeted the new arrival with a noted lack of enthusiasm.

'Darling, you can do better than that,' she reproached him. 'How about a kiss?'

The smell of French perfume was eye-watering as she wobbled past Sandy on heels that were better suited to a cat-walk and flung her arms around Ben's neck. 'I've arrived,' she announced.

'So I can see.' Ben put a hand over hers as if to ease her embrace.

Sandy rolled his eyes at Fleur, then raised his voice. 'Hello, Rebecca. I've arrived too.'

'Sandy.' Rebecca acknowledged his presence with a smile that didn't reach her eyes. 'I thought you were due later in the week.'

'I wish everybody would stop saying that,' he complained. 'It's making me feel unwelcome.'

'If the cap fits,' Rebecca responded with a tinkling laugh. 'Heavens, don't look at me like that, Sandy. It was only a joke.'

'Clearly we don't share the same sense of humour,' he replied.

Fleur wondered if she could slip away unnoticed. When it was announced that the seriously successful novelist Rebecca Ebony was to appear at the festival as part of their line-up of guest speakers, Fleur had been flabbergasted.

'We're doing living history,' she had protested. 'Shopping and boardroom shenanigans are more her thing, aren't they?'

'I know she writes airport novels,' Yvette said, putting on her best soothing voice, 'but she'll draw in the crowds, and we want to put this festival on the map. The sponsors are all for it. There's always a huge queue for her book signings, and I thought with fathers and children having a wonderful time on the battlefields, the mothers could relax with a cup of coffee and listen to her talk without wondering what their offspring are up to.'

'Yes, but why is she coming?' Fleur demanded. 'History, living or otherwise, is hardly her thing, is it? Even with the promise of coffee and cake and girly chat.'

'Keep it under your hat.' Yvette cast a glance over her shoulder as if to make sure they weren't being overheard. Following her example, Fleur leaned in closer. 'The rumour is, she and Ben Salt have an understanding.'

'You mean a romantic one?' Fleur could hardly believe what she was hearing.

'That's what I've been led to believe.'

'But he's an action man.'

'It takes all sorts.'

'And we have to put up with her at the festival to keep him happy?'

'I wouldn't put it quite like that,' Yvette objected.

'It all boils down to much the same thing doesn't it?'

'I'm sure we won't see much of her. She doesn't do muddy fields, and I can't see her indulging in much medieval revelry. As long as we're all on parade for her talk, everything should be fine.'

'I hope you're right,' Fleur had responded.

Looking at Rebecca Ebony now, Fleur suspected Yvette had made a serious error of judgement. At school, Fleur had never been a part of Becky's gang. Becky had always resented Fleur's popularity, and when Mr Denman had fallen from grace she had made Fleur suffer. Yvette, her only friend, had stood by her, but they were two against ten.

Not one to give in without a fight, Fleur's revenge had been to have Yvette cause a distraction at the front of the geography class while Fleur, seizing her chance, hacked off half of Becky's ponytail. Becky's hair was her pride and joy, and she didn't take kindly to being an object of ridicule. Becky had vowed never to forgive her.

The scene now played out in Fleur's mind as she remembered everyone laughing at Becky, and how one or two of her classmates were brave enough to taunt her for having lost her crowning glory, comparing her new look to that of a tramp.

'I wouldn't have thought this sort of thing was your scene, Ben,' Rebecca said, continuing to ignore Sandy. 'We're seriously into Hicksville.'

'I happen to live here,' Ben pointed out, 'and I like it.'

'I told my agent if it hadn't been for your special request I wouldn't have come within a hundred miles of this festival. I mean, who's ever heard of Ridgly Parva?'

'The locals?' Sandy butted in.

'It sounds like something out of a third-rate murder mystery,' Rebecca said scornfully.

Sandy's cheerful smile was back in action. 'You never know, Rebecca — someone may get you with an arrow before the week's out. Then we'll have our murder mystery, won't we?'

Rebecca flashed Sandy a look of distaste.

'Only joking — isn't that the expression?'

'Talking of crime, I understand the

event organiser is the daughter of a crook,' Rebecca gloated. 'I mean, have you ever heard anything like it? Perhaps there's more to this Ridgly Parva place than first meets the eye.'

'You'd do well not to go round repeating stories of that nature,' Ben insisted in a cold voice.

Rebecca ignored his warning. 'And have you seen that ridiculous female floating about the place in an Ascot hat? She's insisting on seeing everyone's pass. You're going to have to have a word with her, Ben. People must be made to realise that I'm a VIP.'

Fleur stood up before Sandy could make another of his disastrous bloopers and introduce her. 'Best get back,' she murmured in his ear. 'Glad you sorted out the flood in the kitchen, Sandy.'

'Sorry you got the blame. If I can do anything to make things up ...'

'Keep me away from Rebecca Ebony?'

'Now that *is* asking a lot,' he conceded. 'If it's any consolation, from what I've seen so far of the Ridgly Parva crowd, they're more than a match for our star novelist.'

Had Rebecca recognised Fleur, and was she playing cat and mouse? It was Becky's style to make her victims suffer. It had been a long time since they were at school together, but Becky had always had a thing about hair, and Fleur's was still the same distinctive colour. That was the trouble when you had red hair. People remembered you.

'See you tonight?' Sandy was now looking like an anxious schoolboy. 'You won't tell on me, will you?'

'About what?' Fleur was not ready for another major crisis.

Sandy cast a glance at Ben. 'I'd like to say Ben was exaggerating, but every word is true. I'm hopeless at the two-step or whatever it is you do at barn dances.'

'Your secret is safe with me,' Fleur promised, 'and I'm sure Yvette will be far too polite to mention your two left feet.'

As Fleur trudged across the grass, Rebecca's laughter rang in her ears. She bumped into Yvette outside the press tent.

'I thought you were going home to change,' Yvette said.

'I got waylaid.' Fleur didn't have the energy to go into further details. 'By the way, Rebecca Ebony's arrived.'

Yvette took a sharp intake of breath. 'Another one who's early. Why people can't keep to their schedules is beyond me.'

'Then you don't know?'

Yvette began frantically inspecting the timetable pinned to the noticeboard. 'It is only Monday. What on earth are we going to do with her until Sunday afternoon? I'd better go and welcome our star guest, I suppose.'

'You could be in for a shock.'

'And that is?'

'She thinks we're a bunch of yokels.'

'Does she indeed?' Yvette bridled.

'She's already had a set-to with my mother.'

'Bet your mother came off best.' Yvette's generous lips curved into a smile. 'Anything else?'

'Ben Salt's kitchen is flooded.'

'I heard about that, but it's not my problem.'

'This one is.'

'What one?'

'Rebecca Ebony is Becky the Bully.'

Yvette paled. 'Are you absolutely sure?'

'I wish I was wrong. I don't understand why neither of us recognised her from her publicity photo.'

'Did she recognise you?'

'If she did, she isn't saying. But with my hair …'

'There's no disguising your flaming locks,' Yvette agreed.

'She also mentioned that I was the daughter of a crook.'

'Then she did recognise you.' Yvette looked ready to explode.

'Not in so many words, but I think it was a veiled threat.'

Yvette drummed her fingers on the table, a sign that she was disturbed. 'It's a setback, I will acknowledge, but I'm sure we're all professional enough to overcome a little local difficulty.'

'I hope so, but I seem to recall Becky saying she'd get even with me if it was the last thing she ever did.'

'We were children.'

'Becky was a teenager with attitude and I had just cut off her hair.'

'Put like that, I suppose you wouldn't like to take two weeks' holiday, would you?'

'Not right now.'

'In that case, we're going to have to grit our teeth and get on with it.' Yvette removed a sheet of paper from her clipboard and handed it over to Fleur.

'What's this?'

'Becky's — sorry, Rebecca's list of personal requirements. In another life I assured her agent that whatever she wants she can have.'

'Within reason,' Fleur protested, scanning the list.

'If we keep her sweet, she may forget about revenge and all that other stuff.'

'I'm not sure if the village shop's heard of edamame beans. Neither have I, come to that.'

'They're immature soya beans. Especially good for females, so I'm told.'

'Then bring 'em on.' Fleur pocketed the list. 'Will *Rebecca* —' Fleur emphasised the name. '— settle for a tin of baked beans if Arthur's fresh out of edamame beans?'

'Don't rattle her cage.' Yvette used the tone of voice indicating she was the boss.

'Whatever you say,' Fleur backtracked.

'Where did you say she was?'

'With Ben Salt.'

'I mean it, Fleur. Try not to upset her. She's a big draw.'

'She's a big something else too, and you're beginning to sound like my mother.' Fleur was unable to shake off her feeling of apprehension. Seeing Becky again had seriously unsettled her.

'According to you, I could do a lot worse,' Yvette responded. 'Now, are we done?'

Yvette tied back the flap of the tent, indicating the day's briefing meeting was at an end.

'What's all this about you and Sandy

wanting to tango to the Hayseeds?' asked Fleur, in an effort to lighten the atmosphere as they walked across the grass.

'What on earth are you talking about?'

A little boy with his face painted in the colours of a tiger lost control of his ice cream and narrowly missed spilling it down Yvette's trousers. 'Look out!' he shouted. The cornet landed with a dull plop in a puddle of mud.

'Bad luck,' Fleur sympathised as his lip wobbled with disappointment. 'Strawberry ripple's my favourite too.'

'Deal with it,' Yvette instructed, striding away from Fleur.

Ben ambled up from the direction of the tea tent. 'I saw it all,' he said to the boy, 'and it wasn't your fault. Here, get another one.' He gave him a coin. 'Only this time take more care. I'm not paying for a third.' Beaming his thanks, the boy raced off.

'That wasn't necessary, but thank you,' Fleur said.

Before Ben could reply, an arrow flew past Fleur's ear and landed on the grass.

'Sorry,' another child muttered as he scuttled past Fleur to pick it up. 'I know you showed me what to do with my weights and how to point the flight in the right direction, Fleur, but it's not easy. Can you do it?' he asked Ben hopefully.

'Sorry, I can't,' Ben admitted.

'Then what are you doing here?' the boy asked.

'Good question,' Ben responded with a rueful smile. 'Why don't you ask your ice-cream-eating friend if he can help?'

The boy charged off.

'Look, about that business with Rebecca —' Ben began.

A security guard created another interruption. 'Fleur,' he said, 'I'm off duty now. Would you like a lift? Yvette said something about a list that needs delivering.'

'Thanks, Jack. If you're going by the village store?'

'Consider it done. By the way, what's all this about you getting into trouble for flooding Mr Salt's kitchen? Is it true he's going to make you pay for the damage?'

'It wasn't quite like that,' Fleur attempted to correct Jack.

'That Mr Salt sounds a right miserable customer. All that's needed is a mop and a bit of elbow grease — job done.' He smiled at Ben. 'Hi — Jack Saunders. Where's your pass?'

'I, er, I'll sort something out,' Ben assured him.

'See that you do. You're supposed to wear it at all times. It's my responsibility to ensure the safety of everyone on site.'

Fleur couldn't quite see how the wearing of a pass would make Ben any safer, but she let Jack have his moment of authority. He was a dedicated member of the team and she didn't want his enthusiasm dampened.

'See you in the car park in five minutes, Fleur?'

'I had no idea hosting an outdoor festival would be such a challenge,' Ben said once Jack was out of earshot.

'This is lightweight,' Fleur assured him. 'Wait until things really get going.'

Ben shifted his feet to avoid standing

in a pool of melting strawberry ice cream. 'If things are going to get bad, I wonder if someone would lend me a suit of armour.'

'Why?'

'Being informed that I'm useless with a bow and arrow, that I have no place in my own field, and that I'm a menace to security, all in the space of one minute, doesn't build up my confidence.'

'You can't complain if people don't recognise you. You like being incognito. There's a price to pay for everything.' Fleur glanced at her watch. 'I must get on.'

'Before you go …' Ben put out a hand to detain her.

Fleur raised an enquiring eyebrow. 'What?'

'Rebecca.'

Fleur's heart sank. 'What about her?' she asked in a guarded voice.

'She can be outspoken on occasions.'

'I've been called far worse than the daughter of a crook,' Fleur challenged Ben, her eyes cool as the Atlantic. 'These days I take that sort of thing on the chin, but I'd be grateful if you could ask her not to be rude about my mother. I know her hats are a bit over the top, but …' Fleur swallowed down the lump clogging her throat. 'She's been so brave coming back from the worst possible personal nightmare, and the thought of someone like Rebecca stirring up the past and destroying her newfound confidence …' Fleur ran out of words.

'You have my promise nothing like that will happen again,' Ben said in a soft voice, adding, 'And I'm a great fan of hats. Your mother is showing she cares, and I respect that.'

Fleur did her best to rearrange her face into a smile. 'Jack will be waiting for me, and I want to get to the village store before it closes. Yvette's given me strict instructions to pander to Rebecca's every whim.'

'She *is* the star guest,' Ben pointed out.

'So everyone keeps telling me.'

'Have you read any of her books?'

'Shall we say, her novels have never

kept me awake at night under the bed-clothes. I'll see you later.'

With the sun gleaming on her red hair, Ben watched Fleur stride towards the car park.

5

Rebecca stormed into the admin tent. 'That wretched man sent up a tin of baked beans.'

'Wretched man?' Sandy echoed from his position close by Yvette's right elbow.

'Where is this Arthur person coming from?'

'Good morning, Rebecca,' Sandy greeted her. 'There are dark circles under your eyes. Didn't you sleep well?'

Rebecca ignored him and glared at Fleur. 'I presume you're responsible for this sort of thing?'

'Beans are very good on toast,' Sandy continued, taking no notice of Rebecca's snub. 'That is, if you know how to make toast.'

'I expect Arthur was only trying to help,' Fleur said, doing her best to placate Rebecca. But their star novelist looked in no mood to be mollified.

'Nor has he heard of soya milk or gluten-free flakes.'

'And your problem is?' Fleur was happy to let Sandy take over dealing with the situation.

'I'm hungry.'

'Because you can't work the toaster?'

'Because I haven't had any breakfast.'

'I wondered why you were so grumpy.'

'How anyone expects me to speak on an empty stomach, I don't know.'

Fleur opened her mouth to protest that Rebecca wasn't scheduled to speak until the weekend, but catching a warning glance from Yvette, she stayed silent. Rebecca was up to her old tricks. She held all the aces. One protest from Fleur and Rebecca would 'out' her to those at the festival who had no idea of her past.

'Would you like me to make you some toast?' Fleur offered. She hated having to be subservient to her old foe but she had no choice.

'Certainly not.' Sandy held no such inhibitions. 'Your bread's got too much wheat in it, Fleur, for Rebecca's tastes.'

'Sorry?' Rebecca flashed her eyes in his direction. 'Did you say something?'

'Fleur's got enough to do without making your breakfast.'

Rebecca's mouth tightened. 'Judging from her performance last night, I'd say Fleur has plenty of energy for everything. Didn't you notice? Or were you too busy trying to convince Yvette that you could dance?'

'Now hold on.' Sandy sounded unusually annoyed. 'I know I'm not the world's best dancer ...'

'You said it.' Rebecca smiled sweetly.

'But at least I gave it a try.'

'And you did very well,' Yvette said, soothing his ruffled feathers, which earned a grateful smile from Sandy.

For her part, Fleur didn't trust herself to speak. Rebecca had arrived late for the barn dance, wearing totally unsuitable heels. After pausing to ensure everyone had noticed her presence, she entered to whoops of delight from the Hayseeds' fan club. They were always generous with their applause, and soon one of them had grabbed Rebecca by the arm and insisted she make up a foursome.

Rebecca had joined in the reels with enthusiasm, but her smile had slipped the moment Ben leapt onto the stage and seized the microphone. Anxious to maintain good public relations with their host, Fleur, who had been doing the vocals, made no protest. Eventually Abe took over the melody with his guitar solo, and Ben guided Fleur expertly around the stage in time to the music. Unlike Sandy, he proved to be a good dancer, and she enjoyed the sensation of his arm around her waist as they moved in time to Abe's slow accompaniment. When Abe struck the final chord and Ben released Fleur, she caught the expression on Rebecca's face.

Rebecca had clapped as wildly as everyone else, but her dark eyes flashed with malice. Fleur stayed out of Ben's way for the rest of the evening, but the damage was done. Rebecca would get her revenge, but for the moment it seemed she was content to keep Fleur on tenterhooks.

'Right, well, I'll leave you to sort things out here, Fleur. Time I did the rounds,' Yvette said, gathering up her paperwork. 'Sandy, was there anything else?'

Sandy, who had been hovering around Yvette's desk on the flimsiest of excuses, took up his cue. 'I'm about done here too. Come along, Rebecca — I'll make your toast for you up at the castle, and I'll even cut it into soldiers. I can also do you a soft-boiled egg if that takes your fancy.'

'I only eat egg whites.' Rebecca looked as though she would have preferred to stay put, but Sandy hustled her outside.

'What was all that 'plenty of energy' thing all about?' Yvette demanded.

'Ben's performance on stage last night?' Fleur replied.

Yvette pulled a face. 'What can Ben have been thinking of?'

'Search me,' Fleur replied.

'Well, don't go encouraging him.'

'I could say the same thing about you and Sandy. In case you hadn't noticed, you have a lap dog.'

'As if we didn't have enough trouble.'

'Has Rebecca said anything to you?' Fleur asked.

'What about?'

'I don't know. Did she recognise you?'

'She recognised both of us, you can be sure of that. I only wish I'd paid more attention to her publicity handouts. I might have been better prepared.'

'What are we going to do?' Fleur asked.

'For the moment, nothing. Try to keep Ms Ebony sweet, at least until Sunday afternoon — and for goodness sake, make sure Arthur doesn't send up any more tins of baked beans. Tell him if he can't provide what's on the list, then he's to let us know.'

'Then what?'

'Then you can find an alternative supplier online,' Yvette finished with a brisk smile. 'I know you can do it,' she added.

Fleur was beginning to feel that, best-selling novelist or not, Rebecca's presence on site was not worth the hassle.

'Have you seen today's requirements?' Yvette handed over that morning's email from Rebecca's agent.

Fleur cast an eye down the list.

'Work of art isn't it?' Yvette said. 'If it's any consolation, the advance bookings for her talk have exceeded expectations. It's a sell-out. The book tent can hardly cope with all the orders.'

'That makes me feel so much better.' Fleur tossed the sheet of paper into her in tray.

'Now, today's agenda,' Yvette said, glancing at her schedule. 'I've got a health and safety meeting in ten minutes' time, a magazine interview at eleven, and I'm participating in a country dancing display at half past.' She grinned at Fleur. 'Don't ask.'

'Sandy could join you.' Fleur couldn't resist teasing Yvette.

'Don't talk nonsense.' Yvette coloured up.

'He goes positively soppy when you're around.'

'No he doesn't, and we're straying off the point.'

'Have it your own way.'

'At midday,' Yvette said, returning her

attention to her agenda, 'there's a sponsors' lunch in the VIP tent.'

'I'll be lucky if I get half a bag of soggy crisps,' Fleur complained.

'You've got my number if there are any problems.'

'Off you go, and enjoy your poulet aux champignons and crêpes suzette.'

'Thanks, I will. By the way, have you seen this?' Yvette held up a copy of the daily newsletter. On the front was a picture of Ben Salt astride his bike, circling an outraged Fleur. The caption read: *I'll pass on the mud bath, Ben, if it's all right with you.*

'Who took this?' Fleur demanded.

'One of the press guys was hanging around when it happened. It's a good picture, don't you think?'

Fleur had to admit it made a change from the artisan crafts that usually graced the headlines. The accompanying editorial adopted a light-hearted tone, especially when it put in a bit about Fleur's mother also not recognising the owner of Castle Brampton and berating him because he wasn't displaying his security pass.

Keep it up, girls, the article finished. *You're doing a grand job.*

'Unfortunately,' Yvette said with a look of regret, 'you've chalked up another black mark.'

'What have I done now?' Fleur asked with a weary sigh.

'Rebecca Ebony's been on to her agent. She thought her arrival ought to have been front page.'

'It probably would have been if she'd arrived as scheduled.'

'She doesn't like being upstaged by a mud bath, is how she put it. You'd better make sure she's tomorrow's star, otherwise your life won't be worth living.'

* * *

Fleur's attempts to attend to the day's paperwork were interrupted almost immediately by a teacher poking her head through the gap in the tent flap. 'I've lost year four,' she announced.

After reuniting the misplaced pupils

with their teacher and standing in as the moving target on an obstacle assault course, then demonstrating how to light a campfire by rubbing two sticks together, before helping Abe with one of his demonstrations, Fleur was exhausted.

The head teacher accompanied her back to the main site. 'Thank you ever so much. Miss Finch isn't normally taken ill at short notice. I can't think what can have happened to her.'

Fleur kept her opinion to herself, but having the previous day seen the glamorous Miss Finch trying to cope with life in a medieval encampment, she privately suspected the teacher had decided enough was enough and thrown a sickie. Living history wasn't for the faint-hearted.

In an attempt to earn a few moments of solitude, Fleur collapsed on a seat at the back of the corporate tent. Behind her she could hear the murmur of satisfied sponsors.

'Hello,' one of the student waitresses

greeted her. 'Do you fancy a cup of coffee and some leftover nibbles?'

'You are my lifesaver.' A quick glance at her watch revealed that it was half past five. No wonder her stomach was raising a loud protest.

The waitress was back a few moments later. 'Here you are. I'll make sure you're not disturbed.'

'These cheese puffs are to die for.' Fleur's cheeks bulged as she tried to speak with a mouthful of creamy pastry.

'If you're here the same time tomorrow, I can promise you some prawn blinis.'

Fleur eased back in her seat and raised her face to enjoy the last of the late-after-noon sun until a shadow blotted it out.

'Asleep on the job? Whatever next?' Phyllis sank into the vacant seat next to her.

'Hello, Mum. What sort of day have you had?'

'I've pressed so much flesh,' she con-fessed, 'that my hand may never recover. Coffee — how delightful. And petits fours — delicious.' Phyllis made space on the small table in front of them. 'Could we have an extra cup?'

'Of course,' a passing waiter responded with a cheerful smile.

'What a delightful young man.' Phyllis adjusted her new hat to stop it slipping off her head. 'And so helpful.'

'I don't know how you do it, Mum,' Fleur said, nibbling on an almond tuile. 'You could charm money from a miser.'

Phyllis now looked positively smug. 'Today I've sweet-talked an influential businessman into donating a significant sum towards our plans for future school programmes.' She waved a slip of paper under Fleur's nose. 'What do you think of that?'

Fleur could hardly believe the number of noughts on the cheque. When it came to fundraising, Phyllis was in a class of her own.

'I've also persuaded Yvette to let you have the evening off.'

'What about my paperwork?' Fleur protested, remembering her abandoned pile of forms.

'We need you in fighting form for the rest of the week. You've been working non-stop and deserve some down time. I told Yvette I wasn't in the mood for negotiation. So when you've finished that highly calorie-laden chocolate thing you're demolishing with such relish, we'll be on our way home for a girls' night in.'

'I can't abandon ship halfway through the day.'

'Of course you can.' Phyllis smiled under the brim of her outrageous hat. 'What I have in mind is supper on a tray in front of the TV, then a long hot soak in the bathtub, followed by an early night. How does that grab you?'

Fleur ran out of arguments. 'It grabs me very well.'

'That's my girl. Now come on before someone thinks up a reason for you to stay on.'

★   ★   ★

Fleur sank into a steam-scented bubble bath and squeezed her lavender-and-mint-scented sponge.

From her haze of essential oils Fleur heard her mother call up the stairs 'Sorry, darling.'

'Hm?' Fleur opened one eye.

'Emergency at the village hall. Some of the festival protesters have infiltrated a council meeting. I'd better go and see what it's all about. I won't be long.'

Fleur murmured a drowsy response before emerging from the bath twenty minutes later and towelling herself dry. She enrobed her head in a fluffy towel and switched on the hair dryer. It was amazing what a night off did for morale. She now felt ready to face the world — and that included Rebecca Ebony.

Sitting on the edge of her bed, she checked her mobile phone for messages. There were several missed calls. She clicked on the first one.

'Fleur? Yvette here. Where are you?'

The next one was much in the same vein.

'Fleur?' Yvette's voice was now panic-stricken. 'We have an emergency.'

Downstairs Fleur heard the front door

slam. Her mother's feet pounded the stairs.

'Darling — I was in the village hall when the news came through.' Phyllis Denman paused in the doorway, her hand on her chest as she caught her breath. 'You'll never guess what's happened.'

6

Fleur grabbed a young volunteer's elbow. 'Where's the catering tent?'

He grinned at her. 'Halfway up the motorway?'

'What?' she shrieked.

'Gotta go. I'm doing emergency supplies. Great barbecue. Ben Salt is way beyond brilliant.'

Through blurred vision, Fleur looked round. Everything seemed remarkably quiet after such a major drama. Where were the emergency services? And why wasn't security-Jack throwing a hissy fit? There wasn't a high-visibility jacket in sight.

'You missed all the fun.' Abe Groves was lounging against a hay bale, munching a hefty hamburger. 'Want some?'

Fleur ignored his offer. 'What happened?'

'Everything was going to plan.' Abe

swallowed the last of his sesame bun and wiped his greasy fingers down the side of his overalls. 'You know the usual party drill — loud music, tables groaning with food, people dancing. Then a deer broke through the cordon, and ...' He shrugged. '... took the tent for a walk.'

'Why isn't everyone panicking?'

An organised army of volunteers was filling bin liners with rubbish. In the background Fleur could hear the Hayseeds tuning up. The night air was filled with the sound of stomping boots above the aroma of sausages and onions.

'It was only the barbecue tent, one of those fancy gazebo things,' Abe explained. 'That girlfriend of Ben's tried to kick up a fuss but no one took any notice. Everyone was having far too much fun.' He chuckled. 'The corporate guests were terrific. Several of them stayed over for the party. I never thought I'd see executive types in suits rising to the challenge, but they did. The barbecue scorched the grass but they stamped it out. Didn't do much good to their shoes, but everyone was laughing so much it didn't seem to matter. They're a great bunch, aren't they? Talk about all hands on deck.'

'I should have been here.'

'The word on the street was that you were having an early night.'

'That was the plan, but the festival protesters invaded the village hall.'

'Are they still making trouble?' Abe asked.

'My mother's sorting things out now.'

He smiled. 'Bet the protesters will come off worse from that encounter.'

Fleur glanced around her. 'I ought to talk to Yvette.'

'She's about the place somewhere. Why don't you join in the fun? Fancy a dance?'

She threw him an exasperated look. 'I haven't time to dance.'

'Some people just don't know how to party,' Abe grumbled. 'You know where to find me if you happen to have a personality transplant. Best go and join the gang.' With a grin he lumbered off in the direction of the stage.

Lured by the smell of frying onions,

Fleur headed towards the regenerated barbecue area.

'There you are.' Ben waved his fork in the air. 'Fancy a charred bun and a burnt sausage?'

The chef's hat he was wearing had slipped rakishly over one eye. He jabbed it straight with the back of his hand. 'This thing's too big for me, but Sandy insisted it made me look the part.'

Fleur glanced down at a gooey mess bubbling in a pot. 'What is that?'

'I think the official description is baked beans. We pinched the tins Rebecca threw out.' He waved a hopeful ladle in her direction. 'Interested?'

'Yes, I'll have some.'

Fleur knew the last thing she should be doing was eating baked beans al fresco with Ben Salt, but before she could have second thoughts he scooped a generous portion into a bowl.

'If anyone wants seconds, they'll have to sort themselves out,' he said. Then he abandoned his pot of beans and settled down next to Fleur on an adjacent hay bale. The hairs on his bare arm brushed against the back of her hand.

He noticed her shiver. 'You're not cold?'

She shook her head. She didn't know what she was feeling, but Ben was different from any man she had ever known. Her last relationship had ended disastrously when her partner relocated to Tokyo, taking his personal assistant with him. That had been over eighteen months ago, and ever since then Fleur had concentrated on building up her new career. Men had not featured in her life.

'Right,' Ben said, 'you know the rules. No talking until all food has been consumed.' He thrust a bowl of beans into Fleur's hands. 'No exceptions,' he ordered when she tried to protest.

Recognising the futility of making a fuss, she dug her spoon into her beans and, following Ben's example, began to eat.

She gave a sigh of satisfaction as she used the last of her burger bun to wipe up the tomato sauce. Ben gathered up their bowls and put them down on the grass.

'Whenever we camped out in the wilds, Sandy and I used to take it in turns to cook,' he said. 'Sandy says I'm rubbish at it, but earlier on he had no hesitation getting outside one of my double sausage burgers. How he stays so slim I will never know. I thought poets didn't do food, but there's an exception to every rule.' He sipped at a scalding mug of coffee. 'Want the lowdown?' he asked.

'No one's told me the official version.' Fleur could contain her impatience no longer.

'To be honest, I'm not sure what it is. Jack used to work for a forestry commission and he's convinced a young deer wouldn't break into a compound. They're nervous creatures, and we were making enough noise to scare off a herd of elephants. No one actually saw any animal and with all the coming and going you'd think someone would have noticed a deer on the loose.'

'Then what happened to the tent?'

'It could have collapsed.'

'If it did, where is it now?'

'There's a search party out looking for it. Maybe it was sabotage,' Ben suggested. 'Local unrest.'

'Who raised the alarm?'

He studied the contents of his mug before saying in a low voice, 'Rebecca.'

Fleur paused. 'Regarding Rebecca, there's something you ought to know,' she began. 'About my past.'

'If we're going to have a rerun of that business with your father, forget it. He made a bad business decision. It happens.'

'This was more than a bad business decision,' Fleur said. 'People lost money.'

'For which he was not responsible.'

'Rebecca knows about it.'

'I should think most people here know about it.'

'There's more,' she told him.

'Go on.'

'Yvette and I were at school with her.'

'So?'

Fleur sighed. 'She was Becky Bradshaw in those days. We weren't friends,' she added in a quiet voice, 'and I didn't realise

79

she was Rebecca Ebony. She knows my history and why I had to leave school so suddenly.'

'Your point is?' The flames from the dying barbecue created strangely shaped patterns on Ben's face.

'You don't think …' Fleur faltered, then shook her head. How could she voice her suspicions that Rebecca was responsible for what had happened tonight?

Ben picked up on her hesitation. 'That Rebecca caused all this? No way.'

'You don't know her like I do.'

'What would be her motivation?'

'We didn't part on good terms.' If Fleur closed her eyes, she could hear the snip of her scissors as she hacked off Becky Bradshaw's ponytail.

'I think you're suffering from an overactive imagination.' He waved at a group of revellers hovering around the last of the barbecue. 'Cider's over there if you want a refill.' He indicated a barrel tucked away in a quiet corner, then turned back to Fleur. 'Let's forget about Rebecca and disappearing tents,' he said. 'Do you think the festival is a success?'

'I do,' Fleur admitted.

'It was a terrific idea of mine, don't you think?'

'Your idea?' Fleur raised her voice in disbelief.

Ben grinned. 'All right,' he conceded, 'Yvette might have had a hand in it. And she was right about Ridgly Parva.'

'In what way?'

'It's unique. Where else in the world would you find such a great bunch of people?'

'You're beginning to sound like a travel advertisement,' Fleur laughed.

'Maybe I am. But I love it here.'

'Are you staying on after the festival,' Fleur asked, 'or are you and Sandy going back to America?'

'I intend to put down roots here. Life in Ridgly Parva is a lot more fun than working on a film set. If my accident hadn't forced me to give up stunt riding, I would've thrown in the towel anyway. This is where I belong.'

Fleur stood up. Enough confidences

had been exchanged for one evening. 'I'd better find Yvette. Thanks for the beans.'

'My pleasure.' Ben put out a hand to detain her. 'Sorry we ruined your night off.'

'It looks like everyone coped pretty well without me.'

'You were missed,' he said in a soft voice.

Fleur was glad it was too dark for him to see her colour rising.

'By the way, word of warning,' he added.

'What?'

'Rebecca is the star guest and we don't want to lose her patronage. Personality clashes can be destructive.'

Fleur found it a struggle to keep her voice steady. 'It will give me the greatest pleasure to stay out of Rebecca's way, and yours too. In future, perhaps you'd keep any dealings between us to a minimum, and preferably via Sandy. Now, if you'll excuse me,' she concluded, shaking Ben's hand off her arm, 'I have work to do.'

* * *

'So you've finally turned up,' a voice taunted Fleur as she picked her way across the field.

Mindful of Ben's warning, she did her best to keep calm even though she was seething inside. 'Rebecca. What can I do for you?'

'You think you've done well for yourself, don't you?'

'I'm rather busy.'

'Don't walk out on me. I haven't finished.'

Fleur felt as though she was back at school squaring up to Becky and her gang.

'This time you won't get the better of me,' Rebecca said.

'I'm not trying to. Now if you'll excuse me.'

'Fleur — there you are,' Yvette greeted her. 'Rebecca,' she acknowledged their old school friend. 'Is everything OK?'

'Ben's been updating me on all that's been going on,' Fleur replied.

'Not everything.' Rebecca's voice was full of malice. 'I've only just heard the news myself.'

'News?' Fleur echoed.

'The latest rumour is that this time tomorrow you'll be out of a job.'

'I hardly think it's a case for dismissal because I wasn't here when one of the tents collapsed.'

'I'm not talking tents.' Rebecca still sounded as though she was thoroughly enjoying herself.

'Thank you, Rebecca, I'll deal with this,' Yvette interrupted.

'You won't be able to get out of this one.'

Shadowy silhouettes were making their way past them as people began to head home. Fleur wished she, too, could melt into the night.

'Like father like daughter, I'd say,' Rebecca spat.

'What?' Fleur demanded.

'He took what wasn't his, and you've followed his example.'

'I have never stolen a penny in my

life, and neither did my father.' Despite Yvette's warning, Fleur found it impossible not to rise to Rebecca's bait.

'Then where's the money?'

'What money?'

'If I were you I'd come clean, Fleur. It's the only way.' With that parting shot, Rebecca drifted off.

Fleur turned towards Yvette in confusion.

'The book tent man says he gave the money to you,' Yvette explained.

'What money?' Fleur asked again.

'His day's takings.'

'Then he's mistaken,' Fleur replied.

'You know the rules. If the takings cannot be banked, then they're to be placed in the safe overnight. I've checked and the envelope isn't there. If Rebecca hadn't found out about it, I might have been able to hush things up, but James Day left a note on my desk and Rebecca read it. Fleur, this is serious.'

'You don't have to tell me,' Fleur replied. 'But surely you realise it's a mix-up.'

'Mix-up or not, Rebecca's threatened

to pull out of the festival.'

'Why?'

'She feels security has been threatened.'

'That's nonsense.'

'I can't afford to lose her patronage, Fleur. Budgets being what they are, the festival could fold without her.' Yvette paused. 'She's indicated that she'll stay on, on one condition.'

Fleur didn't need to ask what that condition was. 'This is ridiculous, Yvette. You know I'm innocent. Becky the Bully is up to her old tricks.'

'Old tricks or not, the money is missing.'

'Then ask this James person where it is.'

'His wife has been rushed into hospital. I can't get hold of him, and I can't afford to call Rebecca's bluff. If she goes, then Ben Salt will probably close us down.'

As the barbecue flames died down, Fleur came to the inevitable conclusion. 'I understand. Please accept my resignation, effective immediately.'

7

'What else could I do?' Fleur faced her mother over the breakfast table.

'What we've always done. Stayed to face the music.' Phyllis was wearing her no-nonsense face.

'I had no choice.' Fleur smeared butter onto a slice of toast, then dropped it back onto her plate, her appetite deserting her.

'Who *is* Rebecca Ebony, anyway?' Phyllis demanded.

Fleur had never told her mother about Becky Bradshaw or her bullying tactics; there had been too much going on in Mrs Denman's life for Fleur to add to her troubles. But that decision now made it difficult for Fleur to explain Rebecca's motives without revealing the past.

'You know perfectly well who Rebecca is,' she replied to her mother's question.

'She doesn't run the world, does she?'

'Of course not.'

'Then why is everyone taking her word against yours?'

'Because she draws in the crowds. Since it was announced she'd be attending the festival, bookings have gone through the roof.'

'Which is exactly what I'm about to do!' Phyllis's teacup crashed down onto her saucer.

'No, Mum, please.' Fleur grabbed her mother's hand in panic. 'Don't.'

'Don't what?'

'Do anything you may later regret.'

'Your father's name was dragged through the mud. I'm not having the same thing happen to you.'

'It won't,' Fleur said, doing her best to reassure her mother.

'The festival was going to be our chance to prove ourselves to the people of Ridgly Parva.' Phyllis's voice wavered.

'You've more than done that, Mum. Everyone admires you. Even when things looked bleak, you didn't let it get you down.'

Phyllis squeezed her daughter's hand.

'That's why I'm so annoyed with you.'

'With me?' Fleur repeated.

'How could you have gone down without a fight? The family honour is at stake here.'

'I had no choice.'

'Rot,' was Phyllis's robust reply.

Fleur racked her brains for a suitable explanation that would satisfy her mother. 'The advertisers would've withdrawn their sponsorship and Yvette would have lost everything.'

Phyllis was in no mood to listen to her daughter's justifications. 'This has undone all my good work. Not only would it have vindicated us as a family, but it would have put Ridgly Parva on the map. Some of the protesters at last night's meeting were beginning to think that maybe the festival wasn't such a bad thing for the community after all. Arthur's wife says business is booming.'

'I'm sorry.'

'You've nothing to apologise for, darling.' Phyllis patted Fleur's hand. 'Are you really banning me from having a set-to with Rebecca Ebony?'

'Absolutely.' Fleur was firm on that one.

'But what about the money? Where's it gone?'

'Not our problem. Now if you'll excuse me, I'd better start looking for a new job. I can only hope Yvette will give me a decent reference.'

'When it comes to mending tent poles, darling, there's no one better in the business.'

'Not sure if there'll be much of a market for that skill.' Fleur did her best to sound upbeat.

'I suppose I'd better go and wave the flag.' Phyllis drank the last of her tea. 'But I don't know how I'm going to hold my tongue if people start asking me about you.'

'You'll manage,' Fleur assured her. 'What's on the agenda today?'

'Two receptions. And I also intend to do a bit of sleuthing on the side.'

'Mum —'

'You can't stop me.' Phyllis was

adamant. 'That money has to be some-where, and I intend to find it. Now, where's my hat?'

Putting on a brave face in front of her mother had been a strain, and the moment Fleur heard the front door close behind Phyllis she allowed her emotions to take over. She slumped in front of her laptop and held her head in her hands. Getting another job would not be easy. Fleur knew from past experience that potential employers ran in-depth back-ground checks on job seekers, and once they found out about her father they wouldn't be interested in her applica-tion. Yvette had offered Fleur her current position because they had been friends at school. Fleur knew she wouldn't get that lucky again.

She straightened her shoulders. Feeling sorry for oneself was not the way forward, and she knew she'd never hear the end of it from Phyllis if she gave way to such negativity. She powered up her laptop. The first thing to do was update her CV. Tapping away at the keyboard, she did so, and then filled out some online applications. She didn't hold out much hope that any of them would be successful, but she couldn't sit around doing nothing all day.

The throb of a biplane overhead drew her attention to the day's festival programme, which was still pinned to her noticeboard. Amateur air ace Piers Mitchell was booked to appear at eleven hundred hours. It seemed he at least had turned up on schedule. She smiled as she imagined the challenge Piers would have on his hands trying to stop hordes of excited children from clambering over the wings of his restored aircraft.

Piers had been another coup. Due to a last-minute cancellation, he'd been able to accept Yvette's invitation to attend the festival to show off his legendary flying machine. After a busy career training pilots, he'd turned his attention to restoring old aircraft. He had discovered the biplane hidden away in a disused hangar in deepest Africa, a shadow of its former self. It had been used for crop-spraying duties and then quite simply forgotten about. After extensive negotiations and monumental amounts of official paperwork, he had managed to have the aircraft returned home, where it had taken him two years to restore it to its former glory.

As well as doing air-show displays, Piers had written a book about his experiences, and it was currently racing up the bestseller charts. His face smiled out from all the Sunday supplements and his after-dinner speaker services were in constant demand. To add to his charisma, his great-grandfather has also been a flying ace. Everyone wanted a part of him.

Fleur closed down her laptop and checked her mobile phone. There were no missed messages, not even from Abe. She bit her lip. Surely he didn't believe Rebecca's scurrilous story? She looked at the landline telephone on the hall table. That, too, had remained silent all morning.

Fleur pushed open the kitchen door. She shouldn't really have expected any sympathy. Feelings still ran deep in certain sections of the community, and she supposed this latest incident had caused a resurgence of all the old stories about her father.

She flicked the switch on the jug kettle and opened the biscuit tin. What she needed right now was chocolate biscuits, a mug of coffee and a sit in the sunshine. With traitorous timing, the weather had turned. The sun shone relentlessly through the kitchen window. The garden beckoned. Fleur opened the back door and ambled onto the terrace. The lawn needed a mow and the flowerbed could do with some attention. Pulling up recalcitrant weeds might work off some of her angst.

Finishing her coffee, she headed for the shed. Dust attacked the back of her throat as she shouldered open the stiff wooden door. Battling with a barrage of cobwebs, she dragged the lawnmower out of its winter hiding place and, ignoring its protests, wheeled it onto the paving stones.

'You need a squirt of oil,' Fleur muttered under her breath.

Another foray into the shed revealed a tin of the required liquid.

'This will have to do,' she announced, 'so no more of your nonsense.'

She bent her head over the blades and aimed the nozzle in their general direction. Standing up straight, she swayed, lost her balance, and grabbed out at the bar as a blurred figure appeared from behind the bushes.

'I thought you had more backbone than this.'

The mower was rudely yanked out of her hands as Fleur struggled to regain her composure. 'Give that back and get off me,' she protested.

'I'm not *on* you,' Ben pointed out in a calm voice. He now crossed his arms and planted his feet firmly on the flagstones.

Fleur gulped. Why did Ben Salt have to look so infuriatingly together? He had invested heavily in a festival from which his fiancée had threatened to withdraw; money had gone missing; protesters were doing their best to sabotage the event; and whilst Fleur didn't put her personal circumstances high on the agenda, the festival was currently lacking a liaison officer.

'Well, what have you got to say for yourself?' he demanded.

'What *is* there to say?'

'I want to hear your version of events.'

'You know exactly what happened.' Fleur's fingertips tingled as life came back into her fingers. Reminding herself of how Phyllis would behave in such a situation, she tossed back her hair and squared up to Ben. 'I'm sure your fiancée filled you in on all the details.'

The frown on Ben's forehead deepened. 'I wasn't aware I was engaged to anyone.'

Fleur took a deep breath. 'Very well. To cut a long story short, some money has gone missing. A note was left on Yvette's desk signed by the book tent manager, saying he'd given me the day's takings and asking me to lock said takings away in the safe. When Yvette checked, the money wasn't there. Rebecca read the note and accused me of theft. With my family's track record, I didn't have a leg to stand on. Rebecca made the position clear to Yvette — either I went or she did, as she wanted nothing to do with the daughter of a criminal, or words to that effect. With so much riding on the festival, Yvette couldn't afford to take the risk.' Fleur ground to a halt. 'I don't think I've left anything out. So now you have it. Was there anything else?'

'I've never head such a load of non-sense in my life.'

Fleur was now breathing so heavily her chest hurt. 'So I'm a liar now as well as a thief?'

'Did you know everyone's getting up a petition saying if you aren't reinstated, all the staff and volunteers will walk out?'

'I told my mother not to stir up more trouble.'

'She didn't. I did.'

'You?'

'When word got round about what had happened, everyone downed tools. Rebecca tried to bluff her way out of it, but Yvette filled me in on the details.'

'I don't believe it.'

'Now who's accusing who of not telling the truth?'

A smile tweaked the corner of Ben's mouth. In the warmth of the sun he had forsaken his leather jacket. Fleur did her best to concentrate on the more important issues of the day rather than the way the material of his white T-shirt clung to his toned chest muscles.

'You mean they withdrew their labour?' Fleur managed to stutter.

'Ridgly Parva's blood is well and truly up. One of their numbers has been attacked from the outside and they don't like it. Neither do I.'

Fleur was feeling so hot she wished she could take off her thick gardening shirt, but she was only wearing a flimsy top underneath, and from the look in Ben's eyes she didn't think it would be a wise move.

'Shouldn't you be in Brampton's Field trying to get things going again instead of coming here to gloat?' she said. It was much easier to remain angry with Ben.

That way she could keep her emotions under control.

'Have you met Piers Mitchell, our flying ace?'

'I haven't had the pleasure,' Fleur admitted.

'He's holding the fort by doing an impromptu talk about his adventures. The visitors are enthralled.'

'Look, Ben,' Fleur said, trying to reason with him, 'I appreciate what everyone is doing. But until the money reappears, I'm going to be suspect number one.'

'Did you take the money?'

'How can you even ask that question?' Her red hair reflected her fury.

'Exactly,' Ben said, pacifying her anger. 'You haven't run off to the south of France or bought yourself a racing car, so I don't think anyone really believes you're the prime suspect.'

'Then where's the money?'

'Well it's not up a tree.'

Fleur frowned. 'Sorry?'

'That's where the sea scouts found the gazebo thing. A splinter group of protesters has admitted to that bit of mischief, but they've denied taking any money.'

'You've spoken to them?'

'I was over there first thing this morning, confronting their ringleader.' Ben's face creased into a smile. 'I don't think there'll be any more trouble from that direction.'

Fleur ran a hand over her forehead. She was beginning to feel dizzy again. 'Would you like a drink?' she asked.

'Good idea.' He relinquished his hold on the lawnmower. 'Why don't I shut up the shed first?'

'Fleur?' another voice bellowed through the letterbox as she re-entered the kitchen in search of orange juice.

'Sandy?' She took hesitant steps down the hall towards the front door.

'Open up.' He hammered on the knocker.

'What's all the shouting about?' Ben asked, hovering by Fleur's shoulder.

'It's Sandy, banging on the door demanding to be let in.'

'Then we'd better do as he says.'

Fleur undid the chain and unlocked the door. A dishevelled Sandy strode into the hall and waved a piece of paper under Fleur's nose. 'What's this?' he demanded.

'I don't know.' Fleur took a step backwards.

'I've been writing poetry all morning,' he explained.

'Now is not the time to read out one of your poems, Sandy. Save it for later,' Ben told him.

'Do me a favour, Ben,' Sandy said, turning on him. 'Butt out.'

'Hold on a moment,' Ben protested.

Fearing the two of them were about to come to blows, Fleur raised her voice. 'I've got some fruit juice in the kitchen. Why don't we all go through?'

The two men abandoned their aggressive stances and shuffled sheepishly along the hall behind her.

'Sorry,' Sandy mumbled, and he tried to flatten out the creased sheet of paper on the kitchen table. 'I read this bit of nonsense and my blood boiled.'

Ben tried to snatch it out of Sandy's grasp. 'Hey, that's my petition. You were supposed to sign it, not rip it to shreds.'

'What's it all about?' Sandy asked.

'You can't be the only person on site who hasn't heard,' Ben said, sounding exasperated, 'poetry or no poetry.'

'Jack told me a garbled story about Fleur being dismissed because of some missing money.'

'That about sums up the situation,' Fleur agreed, and poured out some orange juice. 'Would you like a biscuit?'

She jumped as Sandy banged the tin down on the table. '*You* didn't take the money. *I* did.'

8

'If you don't accept my dinner invitation, I am going to have to crawl in front of you on my knees for forty days.'

Fleur was only listening to Sandy with half an ear. Her voice mail was signalling that she now had so many missed messages it was almost on overload.

'Do you think I could have your full attention for a moment?' Sandy complained.

'Sorry.' Fleur turned off her smart phone. 'That was rude of me.'

'That's better. Now where was I?'

'Doing penance?' Ben was glaring at Sandy from the far end of the kitchen table.

'That's right,' Sandy replied, his cheerful smile replacing his earlier anxiety. 'I attended one of the living history sessions,' he explained, 'and I learned that sort of thing was a regular punishment for those who had fallen foul of their important neighbours. Bet you didn't know that.'

'I can't say I did,' Fleur agreed, wishing he'd get on with his explanation of how he came to misappropriate the book tent money.

'Forget about living history — you're in serious trouble,' Ben said, still sounding angry. 'Even by your standards, this is huge. What made you take the money?'

'I'm coming to that.' Sandy battled on with his explanation. 'I needed to clear my head this morning, so I walked down to Brampton's Field and joined in the living history session. But things came to an abrupt halt when people began whispering to each other; then they all got up and walked out. I had no idea what was going on. I asked someone and they said it was because of you.'

'Me?' Fleur frowned at him.

'Support for your cause was gaining ground.'

'I didn't know I was a cause.'

'Whatever, the future of the festival

appeared to be threatened. There were all sorts of stories doing the rounds.'

'Look,' said Ben, 'I don't care how you do it, Sandy, but put things right with Fleur, then get on back to base and start apologising to everyone you see.'

Sandy ran a hand through his dishevelled hair. 'If you'll just let me explain —'

'I haven't got time.' Ben pushed the sleeve of his jacket up his arm to look at his watch. 'Over half the day is gone. I've got to get back. It's not fair to leave Piers on his own any longer.'

Sandy's attention was diverted. 'Piers Mitchell, the flying ace? Has he arrived already?'

'On schedule.'

'I'll come back with you, Ben, if you'll give me a few minutes to change,' Fleur offered.

'Not necessary,' he replied with a firm shake of his head. 'Your lawn looks as though it could still do with a cut, so if you can get that contraption started —' He nodded towards the abandoned mower. '— that's your afternoon sorted.

Then you can sit in the sun and enjoy the garden.'

'I can't sit around sunning myself,' Fleur protested, annoyed at Ben's high-handed organisation of her afternoon.

'No argument,' he insisted.

She was ready to take things further, but Sandy intervened before she could speak. 'Best do as he says,' he chimed in. 'He's running the show.'

Both Fleur and Ben ignored him.

'The schools' programme finishes today,' Ben said, 'so there won't be that much for you to do. When the adult festival starts tomorrow, you won't have a moment to spare. Make the most of your free time.'

'What about Yvette?' she asked.

'I'll tell her to expect you on site bright and early in the morning. As for you —' He cast a distinctly unfriendly look at Sandy. '— you'd better make good on all the trouble you've caused, otherwise our relationship is at an end.'

'Ben …' Sandy looked hurt.

'You could have cost us a fortune. Who

knows what damage you've done?'

'I've probably done good, actually.' Sandy sat back, a smug smile on his face.

'What?' Ben and Fleur chorused together.

'It's human nature. Now we've got over a nasty hiccup, everyone will pull their weight, you see.'

'Since when did you major in philosophy?' Ben demanded.

'I observe people.'

'I haven't time for this. Count yourself lucky you're getting off so lightly.'

'You weren't going to put me in the stocks, were you?'

'Any more trouble and I will — and I'll throw away the key.'

Fleur experienced a wild desire to laugh. It was impossible to be cross with Sandy for long. Picking up on her amusement, Sandy grinned too.

Ben's kitchen chair scraped over the tiles as he pushed it back in one angry thrust. 'Fleur,' he said.

She turned, unprepared for his kiss. His lips branded the soft flesh of her cheek.

'I'll see you tomorrow,' he said, and left.

'He sounded cross, didn't he?' Sandy made a face at Ben's back. Moments later they heard the roar of his bike down the lane.

'I'm not surprised.' Fleur hoped Sandy wouldn't notice her heightened colour. 'You've brought the festival to a halt.'

'I'm doing my best to make up.'

'How? And I don't suggest you crawl on your knees for forty days.'

'I promised your mother I'd give a talk,' he announced.

'On what?'

'Poetry. The idea doesn't thrill me, but Phyllis seemed to think it was a plan, especially as my publisher has promised to put in an appearance. If I run out of things to say, I'll waffle on about my vineyard in France.' He leaned across the table. 'I know I can be infuriating, but I do want to make it up to you, Fleur. Dinner tonight? Eight o'clock at the Maggiore? We can talk in private then.'

Fleur watched him fork up the remains of her lasagne. 'Sandy, my patience is wearing thin,' she said.

'Let me pour you some more of this delicious red wine,' he insisted.

The flame from the candle caught the rich ruby depths of the wine. To please Sandy, Fleur took a sip.

'I've asked the newsletter editor to publish a public apology on the front page of tomorrow's edition with a detailed account of what happened,' he told her.

Fleur's jaw was still tight with anxiety. Although Yvette had assured her during their long telephone call that afternoon that the situation had been resolved, she hadn't explained any of the circumstances.

Sandy replaced the bottle in its raffia holder. 'It was late in the day, and I was wandering around the field looking for something to do when I bumped into the book tent man — James Day, he said his name was. He was in a state. He couldn't find you and there was no one in the office. He asked me if I'd seen you, which I hadn't. Am I making sense so far?'

Fleur nodded.

'Good, because this is where things get a bit complicated. His wife's having a baby, you see.'

'And that's why the money went astray?'

'Didn't I say that?' Sandy asked puzzled.

'Go on,' Fleur urged, anxious not to stem his flow.

'James had received a call saying his wife had been admitted to hospital. He wasn't due to be on book tent duty, but they needed urgent cover, so he'd come in at short notice. He said he'd put a note on Yvette's desk saying he'd given the money to you, only he hadn't because there wasn't time to find you because he received another call on his mobile, and that was why he was in a panic.'

'So he gave the money to you?'

'Yes.'

'What did you do with it, and why did

it take you so long to tell everyone you had the money?'

Sandy took a sip of his wine. 'I didn't know what to do with the money either, because I don't know the combination to the safe, so when I couldn't find Yvette I took it back to the castle. I thought if Ben was around he could deal with it, but he wasn't there either. I couldn't find anybody, so I stashed it under my pillow.'

'You did what?' Fleur gasped.

'It was as safe there as anywhere else.'

'Then what happened?'

'After I hid the money away, I came back down to Brampton's Field to have another look for Yvette to tell her what I'd done, only to discover the place was in chaos because a tent had gone missing and there was some talk about an animal being on the loose. Before I knew where I was, Ben had drummed me into helping with the sausages. I have to tell you, it was hard work. The wretched tongs wouldn't work properly, and when I tried to pick up the sausages and turn them over they fell through the grill onto the hot ash below. In the end Ben took over. What's so funny?' Sandy demanded when Fleur began to smile. 'I've still got blisters on my fingers. Look.'

'Poor you,' she sympathised. 'But I think blistered fingers are a small price to pay for being such a ninny.'

'There's gratitude for you.' Sandy's annoyance was short-lived as he continued with his explanation. 'When everyone had eaten their fill, I hared off back to the house to put some ointment stuff on my hands. Then the dancing started, and people began asking me about France, and the money completely slipped my mind. Did you know I have a vineyard in Bordeaux?'

'Ben mentioned it.'

'You must come out sometime as my special guest. Maybe Yvette would come with you?' Sandy asked, a hopeful look on his face.

'Why don't you ask her yourself?'

'I'm scared she'll turn me down,' Sandy admitted. 'I don't have a very good track record with women. I make dates with them, then forget to turn up. I don't mean to, but I get involved with other things.'

'A word of advice, Sandy.' Fleur leaned across the table towards him. 'I wouldn't try that trick on Yvette.'

He tore into a piece of bread. 'She looks a feisty lady.'

'She is,' Fleur assured him.

He chewed on his piece of bread, swallowed, then sipped some more wine. 'You do believe it wasn't my intention to make off with the money, don't you?'

'It never crossed my mind,' Fleur replied.

'Of course, when I realised that Rebecca was accusing you of being the guilty party because of an incident in your father's past ...' He held up a hand to stop Fleur from interrupting. 'I don't want details. Anyway, I couldn't get over to your cottage fast enough. Am I forgiven?'

'As long as it doesn't happen again.'

'It won't,' Sandy promised.

A buzzing noise interrupted them.

'Am I making that noise or are you?'

Sandy asked.

Fleur reached across the table and extracted Sandy's mobile from the top pocket of his jacket. 'You've got a text.'

'Is it another one informing me I'm a rat?'

'No, it's James Day telling you his wife has had a little girl.'

'That's terrific. Can you contact him and tell him we're wetting the baby's head? I always press the wrong keys when I try to text.'

Sandy watched Fleur's fingers press the right keys. 'There you are. All done.'

He slipped the mobile back into his pocket. 'By the way, I've given the money to security-Jack, and he promised he wouldn't let it out of his sight until Yvette could lock it safely away.'

'What about Rebecca?' Fleur asked carefully.

'She's keeping a low profile. Now would you like some coffee or dessert? The chef does a mean baked Alaska. They dim the lights, then set fire to it. It's quite a spectacle.'

'I'd better not be too late tonight. I've got a full day tomorrow.'

'Perhaps you're right.' Sandy signalled for the bill. 'There it goes again.' He retrieved his mobile from his pocket.

'Actually, I think it's me this time.' Fleur read her incoming text, a look of horrified disbelief spreading across her face.

'What's the matter?' Sandy asked.

'It's from Abe Groves of the Hayseeds,' she prompted when Sandy frowned.

'What's he got to say about me?' Sandy asked with a resigned sigh.

'It's not about you, it's about Rebecca.'

'What's she done now?'

'She's pulled out of the festival.'

9

Phyllis snatched the receiver out of Ben's hand.

'Hey,' he protested, 'what's going on?'

'He'll call you back.' She slammed the telephone into its cradle. Her grey eyes were as cold as a winter sea as she looked down at Ben with distaste.

Ben stared back, a baffled look on his face. 'How did you get in? I locked the back door.'

'Mrs Philpott is an old friend. She loaned me her key.'

'I'll have to have words with my house-keeper.' Ben eased back into his swivel chair and took in Phyllis's unkempt appearance. Her hair hadn't been combed properly and she was breathing heavily. 'I almost didn't recognise you without a hat,' he said.

'I don't know what's going on,' she began.

'That makes two of us. Would you mind explaining why you've gate-crashed my office and why you cut off my telephone call?'

The angry red spots on Phyllis's cheeks deepened in colour. 'It's so unfair.' Her voice was now little more than a whisper, and she appeared to be talking to herself.

Ben now looked alarmed. 'Phyllis, are you feeling all right?'

'I couldn't sit back and do nothing.'

Her composure appeared to have totally deserted her. Her shabby raincoat had seen better days, and her boots were caked in mud. She dabbed her red-rimmed eyes with a shredded tissue.

'Has something upset you?' Ben asked in a gentle voice, offering her a fresh box of tissues.

'You know exactly what's upset me.'

Ben winced. Phyllis's voice could have cracked glass. 'If you're referring to that business with the money, it's all been sorted out. Sandy's accepted full responsibility for the mix-up.'

'I'm not talking about Sandy. I'm so mad I could spit.'

'Please don't,' Ben implored. 'Just tell me what's wrong, and perhaps I can help put things right.'

'I'll tell you what's wrong. Rebecca Ebony.'

Ben's reply was a long-drawn-out 'Ahhhh.'

'She shouldn't be allowed to go around slandering people.'

'I wasn't aware she had.'

'Of course you're going to stick up for her. Well, I'm going to stick up for my daughter — and let me assure you, I don't intend to roll over and give up the ghost.'

'I think you're mixing your metaphors.' Ben offered her another fresh tissue before discreetly moving the box out of her way. In her present mood he feared she might lob it at him.

'I know exactly what I'm doing.'

'Of course you do,' Ben soothed.

'I'm fighting my corner, and over the last few years I've had quite a bit of practice in that activity.'

The ticking of a clock on Ben's desk was the only sound to break the silence that fell between them.

'What happened to your husband was a shameful business,' he acknowledged.

'You don't know the half of it.'

'I know from experience how the press can take against you.'

'You haven't been forced out of your house because you couldn't pay your bills, or have people call out after you in the street.' She gave an angry toss of her fringe.

'You've had a rough ride,' Ben acknowledged, 'but then so have lots of people.'

'I'm not talking about other people. I'm talking about my daughter.'

'I wondered when we'd get round to Fleur.'

'I don't expect anyone's thrown your past back in your face — and don't you tell me you haven't got one, because everyone has, some less savoury than others.'

'Are we talking about *my* past now?' Ben asked.

'I looked you up online. You had some employment trouble in America, didn't you?'

'Contractual difficulties that are absolutely nothing to do with the festival or you.' It was as if a shutter had come down over Ben's face.

'That was impolite of me,' Phyllis mumbled. She lowered her eyes. 'I apologise.'

'I'll make allowances,' Ben conceded. 'You're not yourself.'

'The point I'm trying to make is, no one continually throws your past back in your face, do they? It makes my blood boil when it happens to Fleur. I know everyone thinks I spoil her. I do, but she's precious to me.'

Ben's voice softened. 'She's your daughter, Phyllis.'

'No.' She ripped another tissue out of Ben's box, rubbed her nose, and gave a loud sniff. 'She isn't.'

Ben's smile froze.

'I think I'd like to sit down,' Phyllis said in a faint voice.

Ben leapt to his feet and helped her settle into one of the easy chairs. 'Can I get you a glass of water?' he asked.

She shook her head. 'I'm all right,' she insisted. 'I need a moment to compose myself.' She tried to smile. 'I didn't sleep very well and my head is all over the place.

'Take your time.'

She blinked rapidly, as if uncertain how to go on. 'What I'm about to say must go no further.'

'You have my word,' Ben assured her.

'Fleur is my most valued gift in life. When she came to Edwin and me as a little girl, she was scared and orphaned. Her life had been torn apart, and not unnaturally, I suppose, she had to blame someone. We were the targets of her confused emotions. Things weren't easy. She ran away several times to look for her birth parents, and more than once I thought Edwin and I had failed. We nearly gave up on her, but I'm a stubborn creature and I refused to admit defeat. There were tears and tantrums, but gradually we all learned to adapt, and then

121

we began to love each other. Fleur was emotionally scarred, and I was scared that things might go horribly wrong in her teens when she began growing up, but they didn't. She grew into a bright, loving, caring adult, an asset to the community, and never once has she let me down.'

'You don't have to go on,' Ben said. 'I get the picture.'

'There's more. Edwin and I took Fleur into our home and our hearts because we desperately wanted a child. We brought her up as our own, and every day she was a delight to us. She completed our marriage. When I discovered two years later that I was to have a child of my own after many years of childlessness, I silently thanked Fleur. I'm convinced that if it hadn't been for her presence in my life, I would never have had my son. I have two beautiful children. I love them equally, but Fleur will always be special to me.'

Ben poured out a glass of mineral water and passed it over to Phyllis. 'You look as though you need this now,' he said.

She sipped it gratefully. 'It broke Edwin's heart when he had to take the children out of school before they could take their exams because of all that business with the failed organic farm. Harry, my son, was fortunate; he was granted a scholarship. Fleur wasn't so lucky, but she didn't complain. She got a job stacking supermarket shelves while she studied for her exams at night school. Sometimes I would find her fast asleep over her books. She worked so hard, and when she passed her degree with honours I thought I'd burst with pride. When she got her diploma — you can laugh at me if you like because I wear silly hats, but I wore my most flamboyant one the day of her passing-out ceremony and my hands were sore from clapping.' Phyllis's voice threatened to give out as she battled on with her explanation. 'Edwin wasn't there to clap with me, so I did enough for both of us. I could hear people making remarks behind my back, but I didn't care. I was so proud of what my daughter had done.'

Ben took the glass of water from her

shaking hand before she spilt any more down the front of her raincoat. 'You have every reason to be proud of Fleur,' he said quietly.

'That's why I get so cross when the likes of you and Rebecca Ebony throw her past back in her face and accuse her of all sorts of things. She's always been innocent of any wrongdoing and she deserves a chance in life. What she doesn't need is more slurs on her character.'

'Sandy is as devastated as everyone else that Fleur took the rap for something she didn't do. He's doing his best to repair the damage.'

'Then why has Rebecca Ebony pulled out of the festival?'

'I'm not sure,' Ben replied.

'Is there something you're not telling me?' Phyllis demanded.

'Like all creative people, Rebecca can get a little uptight on occasions,' he said, unsure whether or not Phyllis knew of Rebecca and Fleur's past history. 'She's probably nervous about her forthcoming talk.'

Phyllis made a disbelieving noise at the back of her throat. 'Pardon me for contradicting you, Ben, but Rebecca Ebony does not strike me as the nervous type.'

'Maybe not,' he conceded.

'Haven't you got more control over your fiancée?'

'Rebecca and I are not and never have been engaged.'

Phyllis waved away his explanation as if it were of no importance. 'Without Rebecca, the festival can't survive.'

'I wouldn't say that.'

'The sponsors would, and to keep them sweet we need Rebecca Ebony's patronage. She's box office. Fleur isn't. You don't need me to spell it out for you. Fleur cannot stay on.'

'I also stand to lose if Rebecca pulls out of the festival,' Ben said. 'I've a lot riding on its success.'

'Then can't you do something?'

'Before you snatched the receiver out of my hands, I was actually at a delicate stage in negotiations. I'd almost talked Rebecca into coming back.'

Phyllis stared at Ben, aghast. 'Have I ruined everything?'

'I wouldn't go as far as to say that.'

'You wouldn't?' Phyllis asked, a hopeful note in her voice.

'Perhaps we can use what happened to our advantage. Rebecca isn't used to having the telephone put down on her in such an abrupt manner. It'll pique her interest.'

'Would it help if I called her back?'

'Absolutely not,' Ben insisted, placing a proprietary hand over the telephone receiver.

'Then what are we going to do?'

'Let things cool off, give everyone some breathing space.'

'What did you say to Rebecca to get her to reconsider?'

'I made it clear that Fleur's presence at the festival is non-negotiable and that it was not to be used as a bargaining chip.'

'And that worked?'

'To a degree.'

Phyllis didn't look entirely convinced by Ben's explanation. 'If you and Rebecca aren't engaged, why did she agree to come to Ridgly Parva in the first place?'

'You'll have to ask her that,' Ben replied, 'but I do know she has a new book coming out later this month.'

'Yvette told me advance copies will be on sale this weekend.'

'It's a great publicity coup for Ridgly Parva, and Rebecca's an astute businesswoman. It would affect sales if she walked out. Her publicity people have advised her to think again.'

'Do you think she'll take their advice?'

'I hope so. I'm also going to recommend she does some community participation.'

'I can't see Rebecca building a mud hut.'

'Probably not, but she could look good sitting in the cockpit of Piers Mitchell's biplane, and she could also pretend to do a bit of basket-weaving with Abe Groves.'

'I wouldn't be too sure on that one. He's sweet on Fleur.'

'Maybe not, but you get my drift, don't you?'

'It could work,' Phyllis acknowledged.

'It *will* work,' Ben corrected her. 'And if stories should get into the press, you know the old saying — there's no such thing as bad publicity. People will turn up in droves to see what all the fuss was about.'

'Can I help in any way?' Phyllis offered, looking more like her old self.

'Why don't you go and dust down your best hat in readiness for another busy day?'

'And Fleur? I left her in the office telling Yvette the last thing she wanted to do was jeopardise the festival.'

'Tell her she's been reinstated.'

'Then it's official? Fleur's back in?'

'She was never out.'

Phyllis struggled to her feet. 'Thank you.' She hugged Ben, then kissed him on the cheek. 'I'm sorry I made such a fool of myself, but when I feel strongly about something I have to act.'

'Don't mention it.'

Phyllis released her hold on Ben. 'There is one more thing.'

'Yes?' he asked with a wary look on his face.

'You need to shave. Designer stubble is so yesterday.'

10

Phyllis barged into the admin tent, interrupting Yvette mid-flow. 'Darling,' she enthused, 'it's all settled.'

A shiver of apprehension worked its way down Fleur's spine. 'What have you done?' she asked in a shaky voice. She'd seen that look on her mother's face before. Phyllis was on a roll.

'What every mother does for their daughter. I've looked after your best interests. There's no need to glare, darling. It's unattractive and so ageing.'

Yvette greeted her with a reluctant smile. 'Phyllis, shouldn't you be working the VIP tent?'

'Not in these clothes.'

'Yes — I hate to mention it, but why are you dressed like a scarecrow?' Yvette asked.

'I do have moments of stress, and this morning I was stressed.'

Fleur bit her lip, remembering the heated scene over breakfast when Phyllis had learned of the latest developments regarding Rebecca and Fleur's decision not to continue with her contract as it was disrupting the festival.

'I shouldn't have involved you, Mum,' Fleur now apologised.

'Yes you should,' Phyllis insisted.

'Phyllis,' Yvette said, raising her voice in an attempt to assert her authority over the situation, 'this is a business meeting, so if you would excuse us?'

Phyllis dismissed the interruption with a wave of her hand. 'I *am* here on business. I have Ben Salt's full permission to inform all those present that Fleur has been reinstated. She is not to even *think* of resigning again.' She cast a disapproving look in her daughter's direction. 'And the really good news is, there will be no further objections from Rebecca Ebony. Problem solved.' Phyllis regarded them both with a satisfied smirk on her face. 'You're now both supposed to thank me.'

Fleur almost leapt on her mother.

'When did you see Ben?'

'A few moments ago.'

'Where?'

'Up at Castle Brampton. He's as annoyed as everyone else over what's happened, and he's been in touch with Rebecca personally. I gather her publishers want her to stay on, and she's been persuaded to come round to our way of thinking.'

Fleur was adamant. 'Becky would never give in without a fight.'

'Who's Becky?' Phyllis repeated in surprise.

'I mean Rebecca,' Fleur corrected herself.

Phyllis looked hard at her daughter. 'Is there something you're not telling me about Rebecca Ebony?'

'What's there to say?' Fleur looked down at the letter of resignation she was holding in her hands, unable to meet her mother's eyes. She had never been very good at deceiving Phyllis.

Yvette came to Fleur's rescue. 'Where *is* Rebecca? Has anyone seen her?'

'I have,' Sandy said, raising his battered straw hat as he entered the tent. 'She's cosying up to Piers Mitchell. Good morning, ladies. If you want a piece of the action, it's all happening down by the biplane. Reporters galore, snapping away like mad. Rebecca's in her element.'

Phyllis greeted the news and Sandy with a smile. 'Wonderful.'

Yvette was still looking unconvinced. 'You're absolutely sure, Phyllis, that Ben has agreed that both Rebecca and Fleur can stay on?'

'Hand on heart.' Phyllis touched her chest. 'The only thing that puzzles me is why she made such a fuss.' She cast an enquiring glance at Fleur.

'I have to hand it to Piers Mitchell,' Sandy said. 'He certainly knows how to get the best out of Rebecca.' His innocent remark provided the diversion Fleur needed to regain her composure. 'She's all over him. Sorry,' he corrected himself with a naughty twinkle in his eye. 'I mean the biplane.'

'In that case,' Yvette said in a firm

voice, 'I suggest we get back to work. There's a lot to do.'

'Good idea,' Phyllis agreed. 'We've wasted enough time on this nonsense, and I must go and change. It's not often you see me like this, is it?' She wrinkled her nose as she sniffed the collar of her raincoat. 'What will everyone think of me?'

'Don't worry, Mum,' Fleur assured her. 'They probably won't recognise you without your hat.'

'That's what Ben said.'

Fleur wished her mother wouldn't keep bringing Ben's name into the conversation.

'I'm glad we're all friends again,' Sandy said, beaming at everyone. 'Can I do anything for you, Yvette?'

'Have you got your talk ready, young man?' Phyllis demanded.

'Word perfect.' Sandy sketched a bow. 'But I'm still a bag of nerves.'

'You deserve to be,' Phyllis sniffed, 'after all the trouble you've caused.'

Yvette took pity on Sandy's crestfallen face. 'Why don't you accompany me on my rounds? You can give out the daily news-sheet. Look you've made the front page.'

'Resident poet saves the day,' Sandy read the headline.

'And there's a newsflash about the new baby being a little girl and a picture of the proud parents,' Yvette added. 'We wanted to play down the business of the missing money.'

'I agree,' said Phyllis with a nod. 'The less said about that incident the better.'

'Come on then.' Sandy rammed his hat back on his head and, displaying old-fashioned courtesy, held out his arm to Yvette. 'The resident poet requests the pleasure of Yvette Palmer's company.'

After a moment's hesitation, Yvette linked her arm through Sandy's. 'People will think we're Darby and Joan,' she joked.

'Is that a bad thing?' Sandy asked.

'You know my views on marriage. I'm a career girl.'

'You're allowed to change your mind,' Sandy insisted. 'Shall we go?'

Casting a tolerant look over her shoulder to where Phyllis and Fleur were standing, Yvette allowed Sandy to lead her outside.

'Sandy's really taken with Yvette, isn't he?' Phyllis proclaimed as the two of them ducked under the tent flap and made their way into the sunshine.

'Never mind them,' Fleur said. 'I want to know what went on between you and Ben.'

'You really are being tiresome, darling, but if you insist. I told him I thought it was absolutely disgraceful that you were being victimised by someone who really ought to know better. By 'someone', I mean Rebecca,' she clarified. 'Ben agreed with me. He was on the telephone to her when I accosted him. Actually, we exchanged a few home truths,' she admitted.

Fleur winced at these words. 'What did you tell him?' she demanded.

'This and that.' It was Phyllis's turn to look evasive.

'Go on,' Fleur urged her mother.

'After we'd talked things through, he

assured me there was no question of you being let go, and then he gave me full permission to tell you the good news personally — namely that you and Rebecca are both staying on. He probably would have told you himself,' Phyllis confided in a softer voice, 'only he had to go and shave.' Her eyes took on a dreamy look. 'I have to say, designer stubble gives some men a rugged air.'

'Mum, stick to the point,' Fleur insisted.

'Are you blushing?'

'No, I'm not.'

'You look rather warm to me.'

'Get on with it, Mum.'

'Of course, dear. Get on with what?'

'Rebecca is definitely staying on and so am I?'

'Absolutely. Isn't it wonderful? Now I can't stand around chatting to you any longer. Yvette's right — I must make myself available in the VIP tent.'

Fleur leaned forward and kissed her mother's cheek. 'Thanks, Mum.'

'The best thanks you can give me is to get on with your job.'

'Yessir.' Fleur saluted her mother.

Phyllis glanced outside. 'Ben Salt is heading over this way. I'll make myself scarce.'

Ben was freshly shaved and wearing another of his white T-shirts and a pair of stonewashed jeans held up by a studded biker belt. He smiled at Fleur for a long moment before speaking. 'Your mother gave you the good news?' he asked.

Fleur wished Phyllis had not used the word 'rugged' to describe Ben, even if it did suit him perfectly. He looked at Fleur with questioning eyes, waiting for her reply.

'What did you say to Rebecca to make her change her mind?'

'Her publishers talked her out of it. There won't be any more trouble.'

'I'm sorry if my mother interfered.' Ben's arm muscle twitched under her touch. 'She can be overprotective at times.'

'We came to a mutual understanding, shall we say.'

The heat inside the tent was getting to Fleur and she longed to be outside in the fresh air.

'So no more resigning? Any problems, come and find me.'

'Agreed.' Fleur nodded.

★ ★ ★

The school activities came to a close later that afternoon; and after all the speeches had been made and the buses had driven away, an army of volunteers began to prepare for the forthcoming Friday Fun Day, the prelude to the weekend activities. Huge vehicles disgorged muscle-bound men who immediately began to unload their equipment.

'Need a hand?' Ben asked Fleur before joining her in stacking deck chairs into as small a space as possible.

'Until they're erected,' Fleur puffed, 'they have to be out of harm's way.'

'I didn't realise deck chairs were classified as dangerous creatures.' Ben heaved the last of the delivery onto the top of the pile.

'Health and safety.' Fleur pushed a recalcitrant wooden frame into line with its neighbours.

'Do we really need this many?' Ben stepped back to inspect their handiwork.

'If the weather forecast is to be believed, yes.'

'Right.' Ben dusted down his jeans. 'Now what?'

'I don't want to monopolise you,' Fleur insisted.

'You're not,' said Ben, just as insistent. 'I'm here to help.'

'Do I hear offers of help?' called Abe Groves, waving them over. 'Only, these need moving.'

'Are they for real?' Ben inspected the size of the twin speakers.

'Yup. We're going to test them out tonight.' Abe grinned at Ben. 'You weren't thinking of getting any sleep, were you?'

'Have you squared things with the protest group?' Ben frowned.

'Been disbanded,' Abe announced as he and Ben manhandled one of the

140

speakers over the grass.

'Seriously?' Fleur asked, doing her best to keep up with them by providing a steadying hand.

'Your mother talked them round. Most of them have volunteered to help out over the weekend.'

'Phyllis could sell fridges to an Eskimo,' Ben gasped as he lowered his side of the speaker into the space indicated by Abe.

'Phew, made it.' Abe wiped his brow. 'Fancy a dress rehearsal?' he asked Fleur with an encouraging smile.

'Now?'

'No time like the present. We've got to get the pitch right, and you'll be too busy to rehearse over the weekend.'

Ben nudged her towards the stage. 'Up you go.'

Before she could protest further, Fleur faced the microphone, her heart in her mouth. 'I don't have anything prepared.' She turned to George, who was fiddling with his guitar strings.

'This'll do nicely.' He produced a crumpled sheet of music. 'Good old country and western lurve song.'

'Haven't you got anything else?' With Ben watching her every move, Fleur didn't feel like singing country and western.

'OK, Abe?' George took no notice of her protest.

Abe nodded.

'Then off we go.'

'Give it some welly, Fleur,' George encouraged her before their sparse audience broke into a round of encouraging applause.

To a background of hammering, the smell of diesel and the whine of a tinny galloper being assembled, Fleur began to sing. Abe grimaced as the feedback set everyone's teeth on edge. 'Sorry, can we start again?' he said.

Groaning good-naturedly, the Hayseeds stopped playing.

'How about a duet?' George suggested. 'Come on, Ben, do your stuff. No cold feet allowed.' He took another secret sip of cider.

'How much of that stuff have you drunk?' Fleur demanded.

'Enough to make me not care if we all make fools of ourselves. C'mon, Fleur, let it all hang out.'

Abe leapt onto the stage and grabbed up his guitar. 'Right, if everyone's ready?'

The extraneous background noises faded as the Hayseeds went into their routine.

Ben positioned himself beside Fleur in front of the microphone. 'You're not going to let the side down, are you?'

'I've never let anyone down in my life.' She straightened her shoulders. 'Do you have to stand so close?'

'I don't know the words and you're holding the music.' He slipped an arm around her waist. 'Ready?'

Aware that all eyes were on her, Fleur took a deep breath.

11

'Don't miss the great Charlie Franconi,' the voice boomed from the megaphone. 'If you do nothing else this weekend, read his book, *The Loves and Legends of The Big Top.*' The announcer lost a certain amount of dignity as the tyres fell off his bicycle, and amid much laughter the clown tumbled onto the grass, waving his huge yellow shoes in the air as his red hat bowled into a ditch.

Two stilt-walkers teetered past the devastation their orange and red outfits, creating a slash of colour against the muddy grass. A juggler and a bell-festooned jester raced to Charlie's aid, and soon the three of them were tumbling about while the band played on and the parade rolled by.

Fleur flexed her bare shoulders. It felt good to wear a sundress.

A group of teenage girls giggled and pointed at her sturdy gumboots. 'Ace footwear,' one of them said.

Fleur knew she looked ridiculous but she returned their smiles. They were out to have fun, and who was she to dampen their enthusiasm? The youngsters immediately lost interest in her as they caught sight of a bare-chested maintenance man unloading hay bales. Linking arms and pretending not to notice him, they strutted past, preening in their uncomfortable sandals.

Fleur wondered when she had last strayed outside her comfort zone. A small voice inside her head was trying to tell her what she didn't want to hear: Ben Salt took her way outside her comfort zone. His husky voice duetting with hers had evoked images of nights spent up in the mountains, huddling together for warmth in front of a crackling campfire while nature settled down around them.

'Pitch-perfect, Fleur.' Abe gestured towards the speakers. 'Take five? Thanks, Ben — you were terrific too,' he added.

Fleur was unable to shake off the

suspicion that she had been set up. There were a million other things Ben could have been doing; things that were of far more use to the festival than singing duets with her under the weak excuse of testing out the speakers.

Ben returned the carpenter's friendly nod. 'For a moment there I thought Abe only had eyes for you,' he said.

'Abe is an old friend.'

'So you keep telling me. Do you want to join in the dancing?'

'I'd better circulate.'

'As of now you are officially off duty.'

Eager arms helped Fleur down from the stage, and amidst whoops and whistles the serious partying began. Strobe lights picked up on the facets of the glitter ball, and rotating darts of colour pinpricked the drab canvas of the marquee as the Hayseeds swung into their favourite routines. Clumps of grass swished against Fleur's gumboots as she and Ben moved in unison to the music.

'Whoops,' Ben said as he stumbled against her. 'I've known smoother dance floors. Smart left turn if you don't want to go down a rabbit hole, and if that doesn't get you there's a mole hill bringing up the rear.'

Fleur did a neat manoeuvre around the offending hazards. 'Will that do?' she asked.

'I'm impressed.' Ben's lips were a warm murmur in her right ear. 'Where did you learn to move like that?'

'Are you sure we're supposed to be dancing this close?' she asked.

'No, but can you think of a reason to stop?'

Fleur had to admit she couldn't.

'Then I suggest we carry on as we are. No one will notice what we're up to anyway.'

Fleur wasn't so sure, but she allowed Ben to lead her across the grass in time to the music. Her feet were hot inside her unsuitable boots, but he showed no inclination to stop dancing, and Fleur lacked the willpower to protest. His shoulder was firm against her head and she rested her forehead in the crook of his neck, inhaling the smell of engine oil mixed with sawdust.

'Hey, you lot,' bellowed a voice over the closing bars of one of the Hayseeds' noisier numbers.

Eyes swivelled towards the tent flap. Fleur, who had been in danger of allowing Ben to kiss her, came to her senses with a start and saw to her horror Jack Saunders silhouetted against a night sky, pinpricked by stars.

Ben's body was still firm against hers. 'Would you look at that?' he marvelled. 'It's a new moon. Want to make a wish?'

'Never mind the moon.' Fleur tried to wriggle away from him without much success. 'What time is it?'

'No idea.' Ben didn't look too perturbed by her question

'Does anyone intend to go home tonight?' Jack now stood with his arms crossed, blocking the exit.

'Is it late?' The innocent question from the back of the crowd caused a ripple of laughter.

'As if you didn't know,' Jack replied.

'Sorry,' Abe apologised over the microphone, 'we lost track of time.'

'We'll lose more than that if you don't get going — now,' Jack added. 'The night shift's come on duty and they don't want to have to clear up the mess.'

Several more heads poked through the tent flap. 'Hi, everyone!' They waved at the partygoers. 'Having a good time?'

'The best!' another voice replied.

'Best or not,' said Jack, who was in a no-nonsense mood, 'I don't want the protest group making complaints about the noise.'

'It's OK, Jack,' Ben pointed out. 'Most of them are here.'

'Well, now they're on our side, we want to keep 'em sweet, don't we, Mr Salt?'

'I think Jack's subtext is on your bike,' Abe announced. He strummed his guitar strings. 'Looks like the party's over, folks.'

Fleur jerked away from Ben, overcome with embarrassment and unable to believe she had allowed herself to dance with him in such an unprofessional manner.

'Suppose we'd better do as Jack says,'

Ben remarked, still clinging to Fleur's hand. 'Lead by example and all that.'

Fleur hated to think of the spectacle she'd been making of herself. Looking around the sea of faces blinking in the raised lighting, she realised it was useless to hope that no one had noticed.

Freeing her fingers from Ben's grip, she clapped her hands. 'Come on, everyone,' she called, raising her voice above the general hubbub. 'Do as Jack says.'

'And no revving up of engines or shouting in the car park, please,' Jack added as he began shepherding people out of the marquee. 'Remember the neighbours.'

'Fancy a nightcap,' Ben suggested, 'once we've got rid of everyone?'

'Not for me,' Fleur insisted. 'I need my beauty sleep.'

'Not from where I'm standing.'

Glad it was too dark to read the expression in Ben's eyes, Fleur turned her attention back to the malingerers and hurried them along. Amid good-natured groans about party poopers, the marquee gradually emptied and the Hayseeds finished packing up their equipment.

'Sure I can't change your mind?' Ben said.

'Positive.'

'Then if there's nothing more I can do to help round here, I'll be off.' With a friendly kiss on Fleur's cheek, he ambled away in the direction of Castle Brampton.

Shadows loomed out of the darkness as a crocodile of partygoers made their way towards the exit. In the darkness Fleur bumped into a security guard. 'Sorry,' she apologised, only to realise her error. The shadowy figure wasn't a guard; it was Rebecca Ebony. Fleur tried to sidle past her.

'Not so fast,' Rebecca hissed. Her clamped fingers created an iron band around Fleur's wrist, transporting her back to their schooldays when Becky the Bully was in full confrontational mode.

The security lights painted Rebecca's face Gothic colours that gave Fleur the shivers. She stiffened. Like all bullies, Becky had thrived on being the leader of the pack; but Becky's pack had long ago gone their separate ways, and Fleur had given up being scared of Becky the day Yvette had tied the laces of her trainers together and they had watched her fall flat on her face in front of a boy she was trying to impress. The only thing that worried Fleur now was Becky's obvious intention to make more trouble for the festival.

'What do you want?' Fleur demanded, determined not to show any weakness by struggling against Rebecca's grip.

'We need to talk.'

'About what?'

'Us.'

'I think everything's been said between us that needs to be said, don't you?'

'Look.' Rebecca relaxed her hold. 'I'm trying to apologise.'

Fleur was convinced she had misheard. Apology was not Rebecca's style. 'What do you mean?'

'I can't make it any clearer. I'm sorry for causing you trouble. There, will that do?'

'No.'

'Why not?' The security lights moved and the expression on Rebecca's face changed to puzzlement.

'What brought all this on?' Fleur demanded.

'It's silly for us to go on being enemies. It's time to bury the past.'

'Correct me if I'm wrong, but you were the one resurrecting it.'

With a trace of her old attitude, Rebecca sneered at Fleur. 'I suppose you're feeling more secure now you've got Ben Salt nicely tucked up in your pocket.'

'My relationship with Ben is nothing to do with you.'

'Isn't it?' Rebecca shrugged. 'I don't care anyway, but let me give you a word of advice. Ben isn't the sort for settling down.'

'What makes you think I am?'

'I saw the two of you dancing. You couldn't have made your feelings more clear if you'd written him a ten-page love letter.'

'Is that what this is all about?' Fleur

demanded. 'Ben Salt?'

'Actually, it isn't.'

'Because if you're scared I'm going to take Ben from you, then you needn't be.'

'Ben and I were never anything serious.'

'That's not how you were telling it earlier in the week.'

'Things have changed since then. Look, why don't we do a deal? If you promise not to bad-mouth me to Piers, I won't mention your past.'

'Ah, there you are! I don't believe we've met,' a pleasant voice interrupted them before Fleur could reply. She turned to face a weather-beaten man wearing a sheepskin leather flying jacket.

'Piers Mitchell,' he introduced himself with a firm handshake. 'You must be Fleur Denman. Rebecca's told me so much about you and how you were such good friends at school.'

Rebecca linked her arm through his. 'We were chatting about old times, weren't we, Fleur?' There was a note of warning in her voice.

'You could say that,' Fleur admitted,

still trying to come to terms with this latest development.

'Well, mustn't keep you,' Rebecca trilled. 'Piers and I have work to do.'

'The old girl's playing up,' Piers explained.

Rebecca laughed. 'And he doesn't mean me. He's talking about the biplane.'

'Dirt in the fuel system. I'll need to take it apart and clean it. Rebecca's offered to help. Nice to meet you, Fleur. Come by tomorrow — if all goes well, I'm scheduled to do my Fun Friday demonstration.'

'I'll be there,' Fleur promised. 'Good luck.'

* * *

Fun Friday was now proving to be a spectacular success. Many visitors had entered the spirit of the occasion and dressed up in a variety of costumes, from wartime khaki to Victorian crinolines. Several of the male visitors were sporting straw boaters and striped blazers, and Piers Mitchell's biplane appeared to be back on form and was attracting an army of leather-helmeted amateur flying enthusiasts.

Wearing an oily boiler suit and a turban around her hair, Yvette strode across the grass. She looked Fleur up and down. 'What are you dressed as?'

'A Land Girl?' Fleur queried, looking at her boots.

Yvette pondered the suggestion. 'You might get away with it, I suppose, but it'd require quite a stretch of the imagination.'

'Anything to report?' Fleur asked.

'Only the usual emergencies — cut fingers, a lost child, and two of the corporate wives who have turned up in the same outfit.'

'Serious stuff,' Fleur agreed.

'At least Rebecca Ebony seems to be towing the line. Did you know she spent last night blowing dirt out of Piers' fuel pipes?'

Fleur grinned at Yvette. 'There really is no answer to that question.'

'I suppose not.' A dimple deepened in her cheek. 'Talking of last night, you and

Ben seem to be getting along a lot better these days.'

'It was nothing,' Fleur insisted.

'Didn't look like nothing to me. I haven't danced like that since the school prom.'

'Well what about you and Sandy?' Fleur countered.

'You know my views on long-term relationships. Anyway, we aren't here to discuss personal matters.'

'You're right. The less said about Sandy's dancing the better. I don't expect he or Ben will be around much today anyway. Dressing up is hardly their thing.'

'I think you may have spoken too soon.' Yvette shaded her eyes against the sun. 'Unless I am very much mistaken, the boys are heading this way — and at the risk of sounding like a teenager with a massive crush, have you ever seen a better Butch and Sundance?'

12

'Do we look the business?' Sandy peered out from under a cowboy hat that was slipping down over his ears. 'I'm Harry Longabaugh, better known as The Sundance Kid.' He twirled an imaginary revolver and blew on the barrel.

Fleur was about to raise a disbelieving eyebrow before she saw the expression on Yvette's face.

'Fantastic,' Yvette gushed.

'Really? Do you think so? Ben and I raided a trunk in the attic. We brought loads of stuff back from the States, and last night was the first chance we had to go through it.'

'Wish I'd been there,' Yvette said. 'I adore dressing up.'

'Fleur had her chance to join us.' Ben cast her a glance. 'But she turned me down.'

For his part, Ben looked every inch

the urban cowboy. His leather-fringed jacket and riding boots were exactly the right size, and his jeans were fashionably ripped in all the right places.

'Fleur's a Land Girl on her day off,' Yvette explained with a laugh, 'and I'm the girl that makes the twiddly bits in the factory.' She tightened the belt of her boiler suit. 'I borrowed it from one of the mechanics working on the biplane. He did the oil on my face too. Do I look the part?'

'Yes,' Sandy said with such enthusiasm it caused Fleur and Ben to exchange amused glances.

'Well, I'm glad we all agree everyone looks fantastic,' Ben acknowledged with a wry smile.

'Mr Ambrose?' a public relations assistant said as he hovered by Sandy's elbow. 'It *is* you, isn't it?' He peered under the brim of Sandy's Stetson, which had slipped even further down his forehead.

'Yes?' Sandy didn't look too pleased with the interruption.

'You're scheduled for the lunchtime slot.'

'I am?'

'You agreed to be interviewed before your talk this afternoon on poetry, remember?' The employee looked less than certain as he inspected the notes on his clipboard. 'I, um, didn't expect you to be dressed as a cowboy.'

'The Sundance Kid, if you don't mind,' Sandy corrected him.

'We were hoping for something more along the lines of a romantic poet.'

'I'm not wearing a frilly shirt for anyone,' Sandy objected. 'I'm strictly modern stuff. Roses and broken hearts are not my scene.'

'Of course. If you'll come with me, we'll see what make-up can do. Would you mind removing your hat during the interview?'

'What's wrong with it?' Sandy demanded.

'It may hide your face from the camera.'

Sandy snatched it off his head. 'Is that better?' he asked, smoothing down his hair.

'Let's get you to make-up.' The assistant placed a diplomatic hand under his elbow. 'It's this way.'

'Poor Sandy,' Ben commiserated when they had gone. 'He looks as though he's being led towards the guillotine.'

'Someone needs to stop him saying something he may regret. I'll go,' Yvette volunteered. 'Hang on,' she called after the departing duo.

'You don't think we went over the top?' Ben tipped his cowboy hat at Fleur.

She was unable to resist a smile. 'At least your hat fits.'

'It was a bit mean of me making Sandy wear the bigger one,' he agreed. 'Quite a turn-out, wouldn't you say?' He looked around the crowded field.

'There's some pretty inventive stuff on display,' Fleur agreed. 'There's going to be a prize for the best costume.'

'Who's the judge?'

'There are two, my mother and Cassie de Vere. Arthur's donated the first prize of a hamper of goodies.'

'I hope Rebecca doesn't win.' A look of

anguish crossed Ben's face. 'Perhaps you could have a word with Phyllis?'

'You're surely not suggesting I should bribe a judge?'

'Not a good idea?'

'I'll speak to Arthur and tell him not to put any tins of baked beans in the hamper.'

'Crisis averted.' Ben smiled.

'If we can get through today and the weekend without further mishaps,' Fleur said as she held up her hands and crossed her fingers, 'I'd say the festival has been a success, wouldn't you?'

'Until next year when we'll have to do it all over again,' Ben replied.

'Are you serious?'

'I intend to make it an annual event — with your help of course.' He looked hopefully at her.

'My help?'

'I couldn't do it without you.'

'I don't know what to say,' Fleur stammered.

'I was hoping you'd say that it was a good idea.'

'My work is freelance,' Fleur began to explain but Ben wasn't listening.

'Brampton's Field should be playing an active role in the community,' he said. 'We could hold car boot sales and dog shows throughout the year, that sort of thing, make it a working field. It'll be tough going, and I'll probably regret I ever thought of the idea, but I'm determined to give it a go. Your mother has loads of contacts, and I'm sure she'd want to pitch in.'

'Hold on.' Fleur put out a hand to stop him. 'You're going too fast for me.'

'Am I? Sorry, I was getting carried away. Well, have a think about it and see if you can come up with any ideas.'

'I'm not sure I can.'

'I'm not saying right now.'

'I can't make any promises about the future,' Fleur tried to explain.

'I shouldn't have rushed you into things,' Ben said, 'but don't you think we'd make a great team?'

Fleur swallowed a blockage in her throat. 'I wouldn't want you to make more of things than they are.'

'What do you mean?' Ben frowned.

Fleur tried desperately to make sense of the jumbled thoughts spinning round her head. Her father had been talked into a scheme that didn't work, a scheme that had left her family penniless. She wasn't about to fall into the same trap. Ben hadn't asked for any money, but what if things went disastrously wrong? Like her father, she'd feel obliged to make amends, but she didn't have her father's backing. She couldn't go through all the heartbreak again. Nor could she subject Phyllis to such an ordeal.

'I don't know where I'll be this time next year,' she said, 'and you may decide to go off on your travels again.' She knew she was making pathetic excuses, but it was the best she could come up with at a moment's notice.

'If that's how you want to play it,' he said, and she watched the enthusiasm drain from his face, 'then I won't try to change your mind. But I can't say I'm not disappointed.'

'Please, let's get through this year's festival first before we start making any plans,' Fleur said, attempting to soften the blow.

'I spoke without thinking. Forget I mentioned it.'

'My, don't you look the handsome gunslinger?' Rebecca purred as she sauntered towards Ben. 'Just the escort for a maidservant, wouldn't you say?' She bobbed a curtsey. 'Someone to keep me out of mischief?'

Ben tipped his hat in acknowledgement. 'Where do you want to go?' His eyes were fixed on her inventive costume. Her bodice was so tight, Fleur was surprised she could breathe.

'Piers would like a word with you. Something to do with filters.' Casting a triumphant glance over her shoulder, Rebecca guided Ben away from Fleur.

With her vision blurred, Fleur didn't immediately see Abe staggering towards her, his shirt covered in blood.

'Fleur,' he groaned in a hoarse voice. 'Accident.'

13

'Chisel slipped,' Abe slurred. His forehead was clammy, and Fleur could feel his heart hammering against hers.

'First-aid tent,' she instructed in a low voice as a security guard came to her rescue. 'And try not to cause any panic. Mr Groves has had a minor accident.'

'This is going to need stitches,' the duty medic said as she inspected the wound. 'It's deep and could be infected. When did you last have a tetanus jab?' she asked Abe.

'Don't know.' He was clutching his arm to his chest in a gesture of protection. 'You get back to the festival, Fleur. I'll be all right.'

Fleur brushed aside his suggestion. 'We need an ambulance.'

'It might be quicker to drive to accident and emergency,' said the medic.

'Fleur's needed here.' Abe was having difficulty formulating his words.

'I can't leave my post. The medic looked round helplessly. 'It's the busiest day of the festival.'

'Maria, isn't it?' Fleur asked.

She nodded.

'I'll do it if you can get a message to Yvette Palmer explaining what's happened, and lend me a pair of shoes. I can't drive in gumboots.'

'Consider it done,' Maria replied with a look of relief. 'Now, Abe,' she said, turning her attention back to her patient, 'hold your arm up and don't let the bandage slip.'

With the help of another security guard, Abe and Fleur negotiated their way to where the festival car was parked.

'I was thinking about a new guitar piece and I wasn't paying attention.' Abe was still slurring his words as Fleur familiarised herself with the controls.

'Don't talk now. Save your voice for the doctors.'

★ ★ ★

Fleur sat on a hard seat clutching a paper cup of tea. The clock on the wall indicated that barely an hour had passed since they'd left Brampton's Field. She massaged the back of her neck. Her legs ached too. Her sundress was scant protection against the air-conditioning of the waiting room, and she shivered as she looked longingly at the fierce sun beating down outside.

'Miss Denman?' A white-coated doctor approached as Fleur stood up. 'We've stitched up Mr Groves's wound, but we'd like to keep him in for observation.'

'Is it serious?'

'No, but he needs to rest. Sorry, I have to answer that.' The doctor held up his bleeper and hurried away.

Fleur made her way towards the exit.

'Fleur — is that you?' came a voice behind her. 'James Day — do you remember me? This is my wife Amanda,' he announced proudly, indicating the woman standing by his side clutching a pink bundle. 'And this is Isla.'

'Have you ever jumped out of a plane?' a keen youngster quizzed Piers.

'Yes,' he replied.

'Cool.'

'But not this one,' Piers added.

'Why not?'

'The top wing makes it difficult to eject when you're wearing a parachute.'

'But you *have* done it?' the youngster persisted.

'Yes,' Piers admitted.

'Were you dropped behind enemy lines?'

'My grandfather was.'

'Then what were you doing if you weren't a secret agent?' There was confrontation on the boy's face now, as if he suspected Piers of being a fraud.

'I was training, which is just as important as any other job. You're responsible for other people's knowledge. You have to get it right.'

'I want to be a pilot when I grow up,' the boy announced.

'Then it's important for you to study and pass your exams. It's hard work, but worth it in the end.'

'Come on, Rick,' his friend said, pulling him away. 'I've signed us up for the trenches. We're going to get covered in mud, and there are loads of puddles, so we've got to wear boots and stuff.' The boys raced off, almost bumping into Ben and Rebecca.

'Morning, Salt,' Piers greeted him. 'Take five?' he asked the youngsters still gathered around his aircraft.

'You're not going?' one of them asked in a disappointed voice.

'I've been answering questions all morning; I need a break. See you back here in ...' He glanced at his watch. '... one hour?'

'Rebecca tells me you have a problem,' Ben said when they were alone.

'More of a hiccup, really. I thought I'd managed to clear all the dirt out of the fuel system, but it's still blocked.'

'We were up for hours trying to sort it out,' Rebecca explained. 'In the end Piers insisted I got some sleep. I was bushed.'

'You weren't the only one,' Piers sympathised.

'What time did you get to bed?' Rebecca asked him.

'I didn't,' Piers admitted. 'I'm going to have to take the entire fuel system apart again, Ben, and that might mean Sunday's fly past will have to be cancelled.'

'Can I do anything to help?' Ben asked him. 'I'd hate to have to disappoint the visitors. It's been a big draw.'

'The situation might not be as bad as it sounds, but I wanted to give you fair warning of the worst-case scenario. These things happen from time to time. I'm hopeful I can solve the problem, but with the aircraft on display during the day I can only work on it in the evening after the festival closes.'

'And you must be so tired from your lack of sleep.' Rebecca stroked the arm of his jacket. 'Ben, this man needs rest.'

'Go up to the house and get some sleep,' Ben instructed him. 'Mrs Philpott will make up a bed for you.'

'I'm due back here in an hour,' Piers protested. 'I can't just leave.'

'Do you have a basic manual that I could follow?' Ben asked.

'There are my notes.'

'They'll do. Don't worry,' Ben assured him, 'I'm used to using my imagination. If I don't know the answers to any of the questions fired at me, I'll tell stories about past heroic exploits.'

Piers broke into a grateful smile. 'Can I stay and listen? I could do with some new material.'

'No,' Rebecca insisted. 'You are going to get your head down now. Want me to come with you?'

'I can find my own way.' Piers eased Rebecca's arm off the sleeve of his jacket. 'Thanks, Ben. I owe you one.'

'Don't mention it.'

Rebecca settled herself on a convenient hay bale. 'I'm beginning to wish I'd chosen something more modern and clingy.' She tugged at her frilled bodice. 'I love those '40s padded shoulders.' She glanced up at the outdoor stage to where a trio of uniform-clad singers were warming up. 'It must have taken ages to do their hair. Do you think that style would suit me? Ben?'

'What do you think of a vintage aircraft theme for my next Rex Flint novel?'

'It would provide plenty of scope,' Rebecca replied. 'What are you doing?'

'Trying to find Piers's notes.' He tugged at the sturdy restraints, then coughed as the dust blocked his nose.

'They're in the barn,' Rebecca said. 'I'll fetch them.'

Ben clambered down from the cockpit.

She quickly reappeared. 'Here you are.'

'I was expecting something like a notebook,' Ben complained as he almost dropped the weighty box.

'Piers is very thorough. Where do we start?'

'You could try and get your head round some of these.' He passed over a wad of Piers's notes.

Rebecca sat down on her hay bale again. 'This stuff prickles,' she complained. There was no reaction from Ben.

'By the way,' she added, leaning forward confidentially, 'I have a confession to make.'

'Hm?' Ben was engrossed in Piers's notes.

'It's about me and Fleur.'

Ben looked up.

'I thought the mention of Fleur's name might get your attention.'

'What about you and Fleur?'

'It was last night after the dance. You'd already left and she was making her way out of the marquee.'

'Yes?' Ben prompted.

'We had words.'

'What sort of words?'

'Nothing serious,' Rebecca insisted, 'but I wanted to talk to her. You know, clear the air between us. Did she mention anything about it to you this morning?'

'No.'

The expression on Ben's face was unforgiving, and Rebecca began to wonder if it had been a good idea to get in first with her version of events. 'I tried to apologise to Fleur, you know for the trouble?

I'm not saying it was my fault,' she added, quick to justify her cause.

'Go on.'

'Fleur didn't seem to be in the mood to listen, and things were getting a little tricky between us until Piers came over and I introduced them.'

'And that's it?'

'I got the impression — nothing certain of course ...' Rebecca hesitated. 'I don't know how to put this into words, and you promise you won't accuse me of stirring things up?'

'We haven't got all day,' Ben said.

'You don't think Fleur will go off in another of her huffs?' Rebecca blurted out.

'Fleur doesn't have huffs.'

'Maybe not, but I got the feeling that perhaps she might not stay the course.'

'I don't have to remind you that Fleur is a professional.'

'She's walked off set twice already.'

'The second time was because you threatened to pull out of the festival.'

Rebecca wriggled uncomfortably on her bale of hay. Things were not going as planned. 'I have an advantage over you. I know what Fleur was like at school.'

'An accusation that could work both ways.'

Rebecca paused as an eager young mother trailing a toddler accosted her. 'Would you sign my copy of your book, please?' she asked.

Rebecca slipped into her sales patter. 'Don't forget, my latest novel will be exclusively available in Ridgly Parva on Sunday.'

'I've already ordered my copy. My husband has promised to look after the family so that I can attend your talk.'

'If my fears are unjustified, where's Fleur?' Rebecca asked Ben after they'd gone.

He was now busy acquainting himself with the controls of the biplane. 'She's probably with Yvette.' He leaned into the cockpit and twiddled a switch.

'Are you Piers Mitchell?' a youngster accosted Ben as he backed out of the biplane cockpit.

'I'm standing in for him.'

'I'm Terry, and I have some questions I want to ask you.'

'Fire away.' Ben steeled himself for his first test of the afternoon.

A crowed began to gather around Ben after Terry had strolled away in search of ice cream.

'How's it going?' Rebecca managed to stage-whisper in his ear as she wriggled off her hay bale.

'So far, so good.' Ben turned his attention back to one of the fathers clustered around the tail. 'No, sir,' he said, 'I don't think this aircraft was based at Tangmere.'

'Think I'll stretch my legs, Ben, if it's all right with you,' Rebecca said. She decided it might be a wise move to find Fleur and give her an edited version of her conversation with Ben. She strolled among the stalls and paused for several selfies. Tinny music from the galloper threatened to drown out the loudspeaker, and numerous public address announcements had to be repeated.

'Chaos, isn't it?' A bystander dressed as a French revolutionary raised his tricolour-decorated hat. '*À bas les aristos!* That means down with the aristocrats,' he translated for her, 'and pretty much exhausts my knowledge of French.'

'Mine too.' Rebecca waved back at him.

She joined in a game of skittles and allowed herself to be beaten by a child who looked no older than three years old.

'Thank you,' her mother mouthed over her daughter's head.

One of the media girls accosted Rebecca. 'Hi there,' she said. 'You haven't forgotten your session in the book tent at four o'clock today? I'm reminding every-one in person because the public address system is having trouble competing with the competition.'

A loud blast in the background made them both jump.

'See what I mean?' she laughed as a bugle started up in another part of the field and a troop of soldiers marched past in military unison.

'I'll be there,' Rebecca promised.

'By the way,' the media girl added, raising her voice, 'you haven't seen Fleur

Denman anywhere, have you?'

'Not for a while. I was actually wanting to have a word with her myself.'

'Not to worry. I'm sure I'll bump into her. Enjoy.' She went off in search of her next quarry.

A large group was gathered outside the poetry tent. Realising it was time for Sandy's talk, Rebecca slipped into the back row of seats and sat down. Too late, she realised she had not made the best choice of seat.

'Hello,' she said, doing her best to smile at Phyllis Denman. 'Lovely hat.'

'It's a cloche,' Phyllis corrected her.

'Of course it is. Well, whatever, it's very suitable.'

'Lemon and gold reflect the logo of our main sponsors. I think they appreciated the gesture.'

'I'm sure they did. By the way,' Rebecca began to ask, 'Have you seen —'

'Ssh. Sandy's about to begin his talk.' He came on stage to a round of applause. 'Where on earth did he get that hat?' The audience broke into laughter as Sandy pretended to dismount from an imaginary horse. He held the audience enthralled for the next half hour, and as he finished his last poem about a confused refugee child he even had a shamefaced Phyllis wiping her eyes with a lace-edged handkerchief.

'That was so moving,' she confessed to Rebecca, 'and I don't even like poetry, especially not the modern kind.'

'I can almost understand what Yvette sees in him,' Rebecca agreed. 'There are hidden depths to our Sandy.'

'I have to go and judge the fancy dress competition,' Phyllis announced. 'It was good talking to you.' She acknowledged Rebecca with a nod of her head before moving outside in search of Cassie.

'That was brilliant, Sandy,' Rebecca said to him outside the tent.

'Do you think I'm finally forgiven?' he asked.

'There's one more thing you can do,' said Yvette, who had appeared by his side.

'What's that?'

'Find Fleur. She seems to have disappeared. No one's seen her for hours.'

180

14

'Pleased to meet you, Isla.' Fleur held the tiny fist between her fingers and earned a yawn in response.

'What are you doing here?' James asked. 'You're not ill, are you?'

Fleur brushed aside his concern. 'No. Abe had an argument with a chisel and came off the worse. I've left him sleeping it off.'

'Then you must come home and have tea with us,' Amanda Day insisted.

'Oh, I couldn't possibly. You'll want to be together on your first night home.'

'My mother's staying with us,' Amanda said, 'and she's dying to get her hands on Isla. Besides, I want to hear all about the festival. I was so looking forward to coming. Will you be having one next year?'

'Let's get everyone home first,' James suggested, ushering his small family into the car park. 'Fleur, follow me. I'm the red saloon parked over there. I'll wait for you by the gates.' Before she could protest further, James was making his way down the hill towards his car.

Isla's mother greeted them all at the door of the neat semi-detached house situated on the outskirts of Ridgly Parva. 'Hello, darling,' she cooed into the blanket.

'Mum, this is Fleur. Fleur, my mother, Mrs Day.'

'Please, call me Sheila, dear. Now, tea is all ready, so come along in.'

'I have to see to the baby first,' Amanda said.

'Of course you do. James, take Fleur out onto the terrace. Now come along, Amanda and Isla, let's get you both sorted out.'

'My mother-in-law's a good sort,' James explained, 'but Isla is her first grandchild, so you'll have to excuse her if she goes a bit over the top. The terrace is this way.'

Fleur stretched her legs while James poured out the tea. In all the commotion she hadn't eaten a thing since breakfast, and that had been a hurried cup of tea and one toast soldier. She looked longingly at the spread Sheila had laid out and wondered if it would be considered unladylike to grab a sandwich.

'Sheila's made her special lemon drizzle cake, and there are homemade biscuits too.' James indicated the plates on the table. 'But before we start,' he added, replacing the teapot on its stand, 'I owe you an apology. I understand I got you into trouble.'

'You didn't,' Fleur tried to explain, but James held up a hand.

'Let me get it off my chest, then I can relax. I intended to give you the money when I wrote my note and left it on Yvette's desk. Then when I got my second call from the hospital saying things were urgent and that I'd better get a move on, I'm afraid I lost it.'

'Sandy explained everything,' Fleur reassured him.

'I suppose if I'd been thinking properly, I would've left the money with an official, but Sandy was hanging around and I sort of thrust it at him. He didn't have much choice in the matter.'

'It all came right in the end.'

'Thank you for being so generous. It's been worrying me, I can tell you. I'm glad you're back in the fold. You and Yvette make a great team.'

'Thank you,' Fleur said, blushing.

'I hope to make an appearance on Sunday if I can get away for an hour or so, and I'll make sure every penny of the takings is accounted for.' James stirred his tea. 'Now, tuck in and tell me how everything is going.'

'Could you manage another jam tart, dear?' Sheila, who had joined them half-way through their tea, held up the plate to tempt Fleur.

'I really couldn't,' she protested.

'Then how about some more strawberries? There are a few left.'

'Thank you — that was a delicious tea, but I really should be getting back to the festival.'

'My ladies' group tells me it's been

a roaring success,' Sheila said as James made his excuses.

'I'll just go and check on Isla and Amanda,' he said.

'Don't wake them up if they're asleep, dear,' Sheila called after him, raising her eyes at Fleur. 'First-time fathers do fuss don't they?' She gave Fleur a shamefaced smile. 'I know, so do first-time grand-mothers. It's a disease for which there is no cure. Do you have children, Fleur?'

'Not yet.'

'Then that'll be something both you and your mother can look forward to. She's the mayor, isn't she? Phyllis Denman?'

'That's right.' Fleur tensed. Sheila looked as though she belonged to the group of women who had turned against her family.

'It was such a shame, that business over the organic farm.'

'I'm sorry if your family was affected,' Fleur started to explain.

'I want you to know I think your father behaved like a perfect gentleman.'

Fleur coughed into her paper napkin. This wasn't what she'd been expecting.

'I was shouted down when I tried to stand up for your family, but I want you to know I wasn't amongst those who ... what's the current expression? Trashed you.'

'That's very kind of you, Sheila.' Fleur was overcome by her compassionate words. 'Thank you.'

'Yes,' Sheila continued, nodding to herself, 'your mother's an example to us all, and you've done so well too. Never let things get you down.' She patted Fleur's hand. 'I come from a naval background, and the male members of my family used to quote a more robust version of that saying, but the meaning's the same. I've always tried to follow it in life, too, when things don't go so well.' She cocked an ear. 'Can I hear the telephone? Would you mind if I take the call? It'll probably be a neighbour. They're a nosy lot round here, and they must have seen you drive up with the baby. I won't be long.'

She was back seconds later. 'It's for you, dear. It's the hospital.'

'The hospital? How did they know I was here?' Fleur raced down the hall and snatched up the receiver.

'Fleur, is that you?'

'Abe?' She was having difficulty recognising the voice.

'Can you come and collect me?'

'The doctor said they were keeping you in overnight.'

'They need the bed. Besides, I want to go home. I hate hospitals. I'll be waiting for you in reception.'

* * *

Clutching a heavily bandaged arm, Abe made his way towards the car. 'Am I glad to see you,' he said to Fleur, smiling in relief. 'I would've telephoned my father, but he plays bowls on a Friday, and my mother's out somewhere too. I can't remember where she said she was going this morning.'

'How did you know where to find me?'

'One of the nurses saw you with James Day. She gave me his number and I struck lucky.' Abe settled back in the seat and closed his eyes. 'I still feel woozy, so wake me if you get lost. It's Hazel Tree Cottage.'

To Fleur's annoyance, she did get lost, and waking Abe proved a hard task.

'W ... what's the matter?' He rubbed his eyes.

'Where are we?' she demanded.

Abe looked round. 'Haven't a clue.'

Fleur bit down her annoyance. 'Abe, you're going to have to do better than that.'

'Take that road down there.' He indicated a cul-de-sac.

'But it doesn't lead anywhere.'

'I know it looks like that, but there's a small lane at the bottom. That's Hazel Nut Lane, and our cottage is down on the right.'

After a careful drive, Fleur eventually drew up outside Abe's cottage. 'Can you see yourself inside? I have to get back to Brampton's Field.'

'I haven't got my key,' he announced.

'What?'

Fleur's raised voice made him wince. 'There's no need to shout.'

'There's every need.'

'My arm hurts.' He looked at her with baleful eyes and nursed his bandage.

'And don't go for the sympathy vote.'

'What are we going to do?' he asked.

'I have no idea. This is your patch.'

'There's Mrs Jenkins, I suppose.'

'Who is she?'

'Our next door neighbour.'

'Does she have a spare key?' Fleur did her best to keep her voice steady.

'Mum might have given her one.'

'Stay there,' Fleur said, getting out of the car. 'I'll go and find out.'

A rough individual answered the door. 'What d'you want?' he mumbled through a mouthful of cake.

'Is Mrs Jenkins in?'

'I'm her son, and you haven't answered my question.'

'I've driven Abe Groves home from hospital and he hasn't got a key. He seems to think your mother might have one.'

'I know you, don't I?' A look of mistrust crossed the man's face.

'I don't think we've met.'

'I don't think we've met,' he mimicked her voice. 'Your mother's the mayor, isn't she? Wears fancy hats.'

'Is your mother in?' Fleur demanded, rapidly losing patience.

'No she isn't, and I've no idea where she'd keep a spare key. And even if I did, I wouldn't give it to you.' The door was slammed in her face.

'Any luck?' Abe asked as she stomped back to the car.

'Mrs Jenkins isn't there.'

'Who was that you were you talking to?'

'Her son.'

'You'd best stay away from him.' Abe's head began to fall forward. 'He used to work for your father.'

'Don't fall asleep on me, Abe.' Fleur tried to nudge him awake, but a gentle snore told her the pills were taking effect. She banged the steering wheel in frustration. She had left her mobile at the festival and she didn't have any money on her. She heard the grass verge scrape against the exhaust as she turned the car round. Aware that many drivers did not know of Abe's short cut and would not be expecting to see a vehicle emerging from a side turning, she drove slowly back down Hazel Nut Lane.

Without warning, the car began to shudder. Fleur looked down at the petrol gauge. The needle was hovering over empty.

★ ★ ★

Yvette grabbed Ben's arm. 'Have you seen Fleur?'

He was standing by the tail of the biplane while a refreshed Piers was dealing with a constant stream of questions. 'I haven't,' was the clipped response.

'Rebecca seems to think she's walked out on us.'

'It wouldn't be the first time.'

Yvette gave him a long, hard look.

'Have you had words?' she asked. 'Because if you have, let me tell you I've had it up to *here* with you and Rebecca. Between you, you've done a great job of assassinating Fleur's character.'

'I don't have to take that sort of talk from you.' Ben now began to look angry.

'I thought you were different, but you're as bad as everyone else.'

'Now see here.' He took a step towards Yvette.

A distraught Sandy, hobbling as fast as his ill-fitting cowboy boots would allow, approached and grabbed Yvette's arm. He paused, gasping for breath. 'Sorry …' He doubled over. '… just had the news.'

'Not now, Sandy.'Yvette shook him off. 'We have a crisis on our hands.'

'You've heard, then?'

'Heard what?'

'Maria in the first-aid tent forgot to pass on the message.'

'What message?'

'She had a spate of cut fingers, then someone felt faint — it's the heat, I suppose … Anyway, she was the only one on duty, so she couldn't leave her post.'

Ben grabbed Sandy's free arm. 'What's happened?'

'Hey, there's no need to attack me,' he protested.

'I'll ram that ridiculous hat over your head if you don't spill the beans.'

'It's Fleur — she's in hospital.'

15

'What's wrong with her?' Ben demanded.

'Maria didn't say,' Sandy replied.

'Why didn't you ask?' Yvette's face was face pale with worry.

'Because someone came in with a nosebleed.'

'Where's Phyllis?' Ben shielded his eyes against the sun. 'She might know something.'

Rebecca joined the anxious group. 'The last time I saw Phyllis she was listening to your talk, Sandy. By the way, it was brilliant. You're a natural.'

'All that can wait,' Ben snapped at her.

'What's up?' Rebecca asked.

'Fleur's had an accident. She's in hospital,' Sandy replied.

'What?' Rebecca gaped at him.

'We don't know exactly what happened,' Yvette interceded.

'She looked all right when we last saw

her didn't she, Ben?'

'I'm going over to the first-aid tent to have a word with Maria,' he replied.

'She said she was about to go off duty,' Sandy said.

'There must be a written record of the incident.'

'I still think my suspicions are correct.' Rebecca looked unconvinced by everyone's argument. 'She's gone.'

'What do you mean?' Yvette demanded. 'Gone where?'

'We sort of had words,' Rebecca admitted. 'Nothing serious.'

'I thought all that was settled. Besides, Fleur would not go off without telling me,' Yvette said.

'She might have had no choice in the matter if it was an emergency,' Sandy chipped in.

'You had words with her too,' Rebecca accused Ben, 'so don't go round blaming me. Piers — Fleur's disappeared, and they all think I drove her over the edge.'

Piers looked up from studying his

manual. 'Sorry?' He smiled vaguely. 'What was that?'

Rebecca clamped a hand to her forehead. 'I've just remembered something.'

'What?' Yvette and Sandy asked.

'Phyllis said she was going to judge the fancy dress competition.'

'Right, that's where I'm going then,' Yvette announced.

Piers closed his manual. 'I can't go anywhere with my blocked fuel system, and I've plenty here to keep me occupied.' He nodded towards the group of die-hard enthusiasts still gathered around his biplane. 'So if you all want to go off, I'll hold the fort. I'm getting rather good at it,' he said with a calm smile. 'And don't worry, folks — things generally sort themselves out.'

'Piers seems to be the only one who isn't cracking up,' Sandy murmured, reaching out to grab Yvette's hand.

'OK — Yvette, you find Phyllis,' Ben said. 'Sandy, you're coming with me.'

'Can't I stay with Yvette?' Sandy protested.

'I need you to identify Maria if she's still hanging around somewhere.'

'What about me?' Rebecca complained.

'You can help me strip down the fuel system,' Piers said.

'Again?'

'I did see a group of fans in the book tent asking if you were due to make an appearance,' Yvette said, taking pity on Rebecca. 'If you want to do something useful, why don't you go and talk to them?'

'Great,' Rebecca enthused. 'If I see Phyllis, I'll put her on to you.'

Sandy emerged from the first-aid tent. 'There's no record of Fleur's visit, and Maria's not here either.'

'Somebody must know something,' Ben said.

'The festival car isn't where it's supposed to be. The parking slot is empty, if that's any help,' Sandy added.

'The nearest hospital with an accident and emergency unit is about five miles away,' Jack Saunders informed them.

'I'll take my bike,' Ben decided. 'It shouldn't take me long to get there.'

'Keep me posted,' Sandy called after him.

Ben drove as fast as he dared down the country lanes. His shoulders clipped the hedgerows as he leant into the turns. It had been a dry day and the going was fast. Climbing the brow of the hill outside Ridgly Parva, he spied the modern hospital unit in the distance.

He raced into reception. 'Have you had a Fleur Denman admitted today?'

'And you are?'

'Ben Salt. I'm the organiser of the Ridgly Parva Modern History Festival, and Fleur Denman was working on site. I've been told she had an accident?'

'One moment please — I'll check,' the nurse replied. The computer screen flicked figures at her. 'When did you say this was?' she asked.

'I'm not sure. Today sometime.'

'Fridays are always busy,' she said, frowning, 'but we don't seem to have any record of a Fleur Denman.'

'Can you look again?'

'No, she's not here.'

'She has to be.'

'Well, she isn't. Now if you wouldn't mind, I need to get on.'

'You don't understand.' Ben bumped into another nurse positioned at the desk.

She looked up from filling in her report. 'Did you say Fleur Denman?'

'Yes.' Ben took an eager step towards her. 'Have you seen her?'

'Abe Groves was asking about her.'

'Abe Groves?' Ben repeated.

'He wanted to contact Fleur. He said it was very important.'

'An Abe Groves was admitted,' the nurse behind the desk cut in, 'but he's been discharged.'

'You don't know when or where?'

She smiled regretfully at Ben. 'That's all the information I can give you, Mr Salt.'

Issuing a curt thank-you, Ben turned on his heel.

The second nurse returned to the reception desk. 'Has Mr Salt gone?'

'You've just missed him,' the first nurse replied. 'Why?'

'I forgot to tell him about James Day. That's the man Fleur went off with, not Abe Groves.'

'Nurse,' a young mother accosted her before she had a chance to pursue Ben into the car park, 'my little boy's running a temperature. You have to see to him now.'

Outside in the car park, Ben tapped in Yvette's number. 'Have you any news?' he asked when she answered.

'No one's seen her, not even Phyllis. She's insisting it's all a fuss about nothing. What about you?'

'Abe Groves was admitted to out-patients. One of the nurses said he was trying to contact Fleur.'

'Abe Groves? I'll check out the woodcutter's arena.'

*   *   *

'Hello, Abe. What you doing here? Who's your friend?' A man with a ruddy outdoor complexion clambered down off his tractor seat and peered through the passenger window.

Fleur jumped out of the driver's seat. 'Please, can you help us? We've run out of petrol.'

'Have you indeed?' The man straightened up. 'Name's David.' He shook hands with her. 'Abe doesn't look too bright, does he?'

'Cut myself with a chisel.' He smiled sleepily. 'Feeling wobbly.'

'Dangerous things, chisels. I did something similar with a screwdriver. It wasn't a pretty sight. So how did you do it, Abe? I suppose you weren't paying attention.'

Fleur clenched her fists in an effort not to shout at the pair of them.

'This is Fleur,' Abe introduced her.

'Best thing you can do, Fleur,' David advised her, 'is to take Abe home.'

'I tried, but no one's in, and Abe hasn't got a key.'

'You're in a bit of a tricky situation, aren't you?' David chuckled. 'Where are you going now?'

'Nowhere,' she said. 'We've run out of petrol.'

'I can't really help, I'm afraid. This old

thing —' He indicated his tractor. '—runs on red diesel, and I'm not allowed to use it on the road.'

'It's on the road now,' Fleur pointed out.

'That's because I'm on the way to my field.'

'Can you give me a lift anywhere?' Fleur asked.

'Tell you what,' David said, scratching his head, 'I could tow you through the field. It'll be a bit bumpy and could take some time, but I know where Abe lives, and I can get you there via the country route; I wouldn't be breaking the law then.'

'But there's no one in,' Fleur pointed out in frustration, unable to believe that David was offering to take her back to where she had originally come from.

'Doesn't Mrs Jenkins have a key?'

'She's out and her son wouldn't give it to me.'

'He wouldn't, eh?' David began to sort out a suitable tow rope. 'Here, we'll soon have you hitched up and moving.' He nodded towards a sleeping Abe. 'Looks like we've lost him again. I remember when I cut my leg, they put me out for hours.'

David chatted on as he secured the rope to his tractor. 'Right, are we ready?'

'What do you want me to do?' Fleur eyed the length of rope and hoped it would hold.

'Steer your car. Make sure we don't go off course. Progress will be slow but we'll get there,' he assured her with his bluff smile.

Abe groaned every time the exhaust scraped a mound of earth or they drove through a rut. Fleur's lower lip was sore from where her teeth had punctured her flesh. She didn't dare guess what David's field was doing to the floor panel of the car.

Eventually David turned round in his driving seat and with a cheery wave indicated that they had arrived. 'Here we are, safe and sound.' His cheerful smile didn't waver as he undid the tow-rope. 'Want me to sort out Mrs Jenkins' son for you?' he offered.

'David?' A head poked over the hedge. 'Is that you? I thought I heard voices.'

'Hello, Mr Groves,' David greeted Abe's father. 'I've got Abe with me and a young lady called Fleur.'

'Fleur?' Abe's father shone a torch into the field. 'What's going on?'

'Explanations can wait, Mr Groves. Do you have a telephone I can use?'

'You need to get Abe sorted out first,' David said. 'He's cut his arm.'

'Abe?' Mrs Groves now appeared by her husband's side. 'What's happening?'

'Let's get everyone inside,' Mr Groves suggested as he approached. 'Come on, Abe, put your arm around my neck. That's right.'

'I'd best be getting off,' David said, leaping back into his cab. 'The light's going from the day. Nice meeting you, Fleur.' He began rolling his tractor forward.

'Thank you for everything,' Fleur called after him.

By the time she turned back, Mr and

Mrs Groves had manoeuvred Abe out of the car and were shepherding him towards the cottage. 'Let me help,' she offered.

'If you could open the back door, dear,' Mrs Groves said, smiling at her, 'that would be a great help.'

'Please,' Fleur asked, 'can I use your telephone?'

'All in good time,' Mrs Groves replied as her husband settled Abe into a chair. 'You need something warm inside you. That dress is very pretty but not very practical. I'll heat up some soup, and then we'll have a nice talk and you can tell me what's happened.'

Mr Groves began boiling a kettle for hot water. 'Mrs Jenkins called round.'

'That's right,' Mrs Groves chimed in. 'That son of hers needs a smart kick on the shins. He can be so rude. Ever so worried, Ena was. That's why we were out looking for you.' She gave her soup a stir. 'But we didn't expect you to come from across the fields.'

'Or David to be towing you,' Mr Groves

managed to get a word in edgewise.

'There we are. Soup's ready. Come on, Abe. I'm sure you can manage a few mouthfuls, then your father can take you upstairs. Would you like to wash your hands before you sit at the table, Fleur?' Mrs Groves asked diplomatically, eyeing Fleur's grubby appearance.

Overcome with tiredness and stress, Fleur leaned against the sink.

'For heaven's sake,' Mrs Groves said as she bustled around behind her, 'you're as exhausted as our Abe.' She gave Fleur a hug.

'I have to get back to the festival.'

'No you don't.'

'They'll think I've deserted them.'

'That's their problem. You're not going anywhere tonight.'

'You don't understand.'

'You don't have to prove yourself to the world. Mr Groves and I don't share John Jenkins's opinion of your father. We never doubted Mr Denman's honesty for a moment, and you're a chip off the old block. So not another word.' Her kind words coming so soon after Sheila Day's were too much for Fleur. She leaned her head on Mrs Groves's shoulder and allowed the older woman to comfort her as if she were a child. 'Come on, eat your soup, then I'm putting you to bed. No arguments.'

'Best do as she says,' Mr Groves whispered, just loud enough for his wife to hear. 'She'll get her own way in the end. She always does.'

'My telephone call,' Fleur protested.

'Will wait until the morning. Mr Groves will sort out the car after he's finished seeing to Abe. Now eat up your soup, then you can get your head down.'

16

'Thank you so much for all you've done and for letting me know about Fleur,' Phyllis said.

'Your daughter was most insistent I call you, Mrs Denman.'

'Please, it's Phyllis,' she said.

'Is there anyone else I should contact, Phyllis?' Mary Groves asked.

'You've done enough, Mary. I do hope Abe recovers soon. Now I'll leave you to get on with what's left of your evening. Give Fleur my love and tell her not to worry about anything. It's all in hand.'

Phyllis replaced the receiver. Fleur's loyalty to the festival had never been in doubt. What had irked her was Ben and Rebecca's assumption that her daughter would desert Yvette over a minor difference of opinion, the details of which evaded her but to her mind were not important. What was crucial was her daughter's reputation. She picked up the telephone again.

'Yvette? Phyllis here. Just to let you know Fleur is fine.'

'Where is she?'

'It's a long story and I'm sure she'll tell you all about it tomorrow morning.'

'Then she's coming back?' Yvette was unable to keep the relief out of her voice.

'How could you think otherwise?'

'I've been so confused lately, I don't know what to think.'

'Well you can tell the rumour mongers that's all their stories were — nothing but rumours without an ounce of truth in them.'

'Sandy is actually with me now. Do you want him to tell Ben the good news?'

'No,' Phyllis said. 'I'll do it in the morning. I've a few things I want to say to him.'

'If you're sure.' Yvette sounded doubtful.

'Don't worry,' Phyllis reassured her, 'I won't jeopardise the future of the festival. See you tomorrow. Thank heavens we only have two more days to go. I intend to sleep for a week when it's all over.'

* * *

'What do you think?' Sandy queried after Yvette told him Phyllis's news. 'Should I go against Phyllis's wishes and tell Ben?'

'Only a brave man would do that,' Yvette advised him.

'Perhaps you're right.' Sandy nodded. 'Least said and all that. Right, I don't know about you, but I'm hungry. Shall we go somewhere and eat?'

'The festival barbecue?' Yvette suggested without much enthusiasm.

'Can't you think of anywhere else?'

She tidied up her papers, then shrugged a jacket over her boiler suit. 'I'm not dressed for anywhere smart.'

'And I don't dare appear in public dressed as The Sundance Kid.' Sandy grimaced as he rammed his large hat back on his head. 'How about burgers from the mobile van in Ridgly Parva? We could take in a film afterwards.'

'I may fall asleep on you.' Yvette hid a yawn behind the back of her hand.

'My shoulders are broad enough to take the weight.'

'In that case I'm your girl, but keep the noise down,' she advised as they ducked under the tent awning and tiptoed across the grass. 'We don't want someone spotting us and dragging us back to the barbecue.'

★ ★ ★

The sun was beginning to melt the mist off the hilltops as Phyllis's taxi dropped her outside the Castle Brampton port-cullis. She took a deep breath of fresh morning air to clear her head.

Festival noises floated up from the valley below. She caught a flash of a red and gold saddle from one of the horses on the galloper and heard the whine of mobile shutters being raised in the catering field. Everyone was getting ready for another busy day. A queue of cars snaked along the country lane while marshals directed the vehicles to the car park.

'Sure this is where you want?' The taxi driver eyed up Phyllis's pink-brimmed straw hat. 'The festival entrance is down the hill.'

'Quite sure, thank you. Would you mind waiting? I won't be long.'

Phyllis walked across the little bridge spanning the dried-up moat and ducked under the portcullis, then took a moment out in the courtyard to get her thoughts together. She didn't often suffer self-doubt, but occasionally the dark days of a few years ago returned to haunt her. It was a time she had no wish to revisit. That was why she had to speak to Ben Salt, even if she knew her daughter would accuse her of interfering.

Phyllis straightened her back. Meddling or not, she couldn't stand back and do nothing.

Ben looked up as she tapped on the door of his study. 'I see you've by passed Mrs Philpott's security yet again,' he said.

'I didn't see her,' Phyllis corrected him. 'Your front door was open so I came right

212

in. I hope I'm welcome?'

'That remains to be seen. Have you heard from Fleur?' he asked in a steady voice.

'I have.' Phyllis closed the door behind her. 'We don't want to be overheard, do we?'

'It depends what you've got to say.'

There were dark circles under Ben's eyes and his white T-shirt was badly stained. Phyllis wrinkled her nose. 'What can I smell?'

'Engine oil probably,' he replied. 'I've been up all night sorting out the biplane. But you haven't come here to enquire about what I did last night, have you?'

'Mary Groves telephoned me last night,' Phyllis said carefully. 'Abe's mother.'

'So Fleur did go off with him.'

'Not for the reason you think.'

'Then why did no one leave me a message?'

'Because I wanted to talk to you personally. I know we've had this conversation before,' Phyllis began.

213

'And I know exactly what you are going to say,' Ben replied, 'so to save you the trouble of repeating yourself, I have something to tell you.'

'May I sit down?'

Ben indicated a seat in front of his desk. 'Yesterday I asked Fleur if she'd consider helping out again at next year's festival,' he said.

The expression on Phyllis's face altered a fraction. 'Next year?' She leaned forward with an eager smile.

'Fleur turned me down.'

Phyllis sat back in her chair looking as if Ben had punched her in the face. 'She did what?'

'She informed me,' Ben continued, 'that she did not know where she would be this time next year and that she didn't want to make any commitment. After which she disappeared. So can you blame me for thinking she wasn't coming back?'

'She didn't disappear,' Phyllis protested.

'She didn't let anyone know where she was going.'

'It wasn't her fault the message didn't get through. It was Abe Groves who was injured.'

'I didn't know that at the time.' Ben rubbed a weary hand over his forehead.

'Instead of being so quick to condemn my daughter,' Phyllis said in a steady voice, 'have you thought why she turned down your offer?'

'If you're going to say it's because of what happened with her father, I don't believe you.'

'You have to talk to each other,' Phyllis insisted.

'We've tried that, but it doesn't seem to work. One of us always seems to say the wrong thing.'

'Don't be so negative.' Phyllis straightened the jacket of her summer suit. 'Words are your trade. Surely you can manage to say the right thing — occasionally.'

'I've sometimes wondered about that.'

'I know you and Fleur got off on the wrong foot, but personal differences can be overcome.' Phyllis paused. 'I mean, you and I didn't hit it off the first time we met, but we're adult enough to adapt to the situation. Can't you do the same thing with Fleur?'

'I've tried, but there are too many outside influences.'

Phyllis glanced at her watch. 'The festival car Fleur borrowed ran out of petrol and she didn't have her mobile on her. That's why she couldn't let anyone know where she was. I expect she's back on duty now.' Phyllis looked Ben up and down. 'I've a taxi waiting outside if you care to join me, although you may want to freshen up before you put in an appearance.'

'Ben.' The study door was opened in a rush. 'Whoops, sorry,' Rebecca Ebony apologised. 'I didn't know you have company. Hi, Phyllis. Any word of Fleur?' She advanced into the room. She was still wearing her serving maid's dress, and like Ben her clothes were rumpled.

Phyllis's grey eyes flickered from Rebecca to Ben, then back to Rebecca again. 'I see you haven't been home to change out of your costume,' she said quietly.

'What?' Rebecca looked down at her blouse and then laughed. 'No, I haven't,' she admitted.

'And I'm sure you haven't been out all night looking for Fleur.'

'No,' Rebecca conceded, 'I haven't been doing that either.'

'So you spent the night here?'

'No, you don't understand.'

'Whatever you've been up to is none of my business. In answer to your question, Fleur is fine, thank you. I'm sorry if I interrupted you and Ben. I'll be on my way. I've a busy day ahead of me. Perhaps we'll see you both later when you've had time to change your clothes?'

Rebecca put out a hand to detain Phyllis. 'It's not what you think.'

'It doesn't matter what I think, Rebecca. However ...' She cast a glance at Ben. '... I see I've been very naïve. I can totally understand Fleur's reluctance to commit to another festival.'

'You're holding another one next year?'

Rebecca looked at Ben. 'You never said. My schedule may not be fully booked, if you can let me know the dates? I'm sure Piers would be pleased to put in an appearance too.'

'I'll leave you to it.' Phyllis walked to the door.

Ben pushed back his chair. 'Phyllis?' he called after her.

'As I said, I have a taxi outside, and the meter's running, so I'm sure you'll understand if I don't stay.'

'You couldn't give me a lift could you?' Rebecca asked.

'To the festival?' Phyllis's voice echoed her surprise. 'I thought you were going to change into something more comfortable.'

'Your idea, not mine. I've been making coffee and sandwiches in the kitchen for Piers. He's been up all night. We all have. Hold on, I'll get them. Don't go without me.'

★ ★ ★

'I don't know what Ben told you about us,' Rebecca began as she settled in the back seat next to Phyllis.

'He didn't tell me anything,' Phyllis replied, 'and now is not the time for a private conversation.' She cast a warning glance in the direction of the driver's rear-view mirror.

'Perhaps not,' Rebecca agreed, 'but I don't know when I'll get another chance to talk to you.'

Their taxi joined the queue of cars waiting to enter the festival field.

'I admit I put the word round that Ben and I were an item when I first arrived in Ridgly Parva, but there was never anything official between us and the attraction was a bit one-sided.' Rebecca made a reluctant face. 'My side,' she added.

'What made you change your mind?' Phyllis asked.

'Not what. Who. Piers Mitchell. That's where I've been for the past few nights — helping him clear his wretched blocked fuel line. Can you imagine it? I've been passing spanners and getting oily and staying up all night in a freezing field. I have never been so cold in my life. I was warming up in Ben's kitchen when you arrived.'

'So it was you who left the front door open?'

'Did I?' Rebecca queried. 'Perhaps I did. Anyway, there you have it.' Rebecca waved out of the back window. 'There's Piers. Can you let me down here please, driver?' she asked, gathering up her sandwiches. 'Give my love to Fleur.'

Phyllis watched Rebecca scramble out of the back seat of the taxi and run across the field to embrace Piers Mitchell.

17

'Sorry,' Fleur apologised to the woman at the front of the ticket queue, 'could I squeeze past?'

'Keep up the good work,' the woman greeted her. 'My grandchildren have been here every day. My daughter-in-law's been run off her feet with all their demands, so I offered to do today's stint.' She lowered her voice. 'A decision I may live to regret.'

'I want to visit the combat arena,' her grandson announced.

Fleur smiled at his sister. 'And where would you like to go?' she asked the little girl.

'I want to see everything,' she announced.

'You could be in for a long day,' Fleur warned their grandmother.

'Thank goodness I've brought comfortable shoes with me.' She smiled.

'Would you hurry up?' an impatient voice behind them complained. 'You're holding up the queue.'

Showing her pass, Fleur headed off in the direction of the first-aid station. 'The car's back,' she called over the sea of heads to a harassed Maria, dealing with an influx of minor cuts and bruises.

'Glad to see you're back too,' Maria said, waving at her. 'We've been lost without you.'

'Fleur.' Yvette leapt to her feet from behind her desk in the admin tent and flung her arms around her neck. 'Are you OK?'

'Of course I am. What's brought all this on? You're not normally this pleased to see me.'

'It's complicated.'

'You might as well hit me with it now, otherwise I'll only get an unreliable version of events from dubious sources.'

'The buzz was, you weren't coming back.'

'I thought something like that might happen,' Fleur admitted.

Yvette was now looking most uncomfortable. 'You can't blame us for thinking the worst. You've got history. You've walked out twice before.'

'That's not how I see it.' Fleur was prepared to stand her ground.

'You did fall out with Ben and Rebecca. Tents have ears,' Yvette explained. 'Anyway, no one knew where you were. Someone said you were seriously ill in hospital; then I heard you'd eloped with Abe Groves.'

Before Fleur could react, another pair of arms was flung around her neck. She staggered backwards as a smacking kiss was delivered to her left ear.

'Let me go,' she croaked.

'We thought you weren't coming back,' Sandy said with a cheerful smile.

'We've done that bit, and would you mind moving on? It's very cramped in here.' Yvette tried unsuccessfully to shoo Sandy out of the tent.

'Ben's been saying things like he didn't care where you were, which was a pack of lies,' Sandy said. 'I'm his oldest friend.

He can't pull the wool over my eyes.'

'Sandy, go and do something useful,' Yvette insisted.

'There's no need to be so rough,' he complained as she manhandled him outside.

'I did leave a message,' Fleur explained after he'd gone.

'I know that now, but never mind. Save your story for a long winter's evening.' Yvette turned her attention to the day's timetable. 'We've got VIPs crawling all over the place. Jack and his security team are going into meltdown. The media tent staff can't track down half of their guests because they're all behaving like overgrown children fighting in the trenches and re-enacting battles. We even discovered one chief executive riding on the galloper. He said he hadn't had so much fun in years.'

'What do you want me to do?'

'Work a miracle?' Yvette suggested.

'I'll do my best.'

'And no going off anywhere without telling at least three people. I can't go through another afternoon like yesterday. I nearly threw in the towel.'

'Yes, ma'am.'

'Also,' Yvette added, fiddling with a stray paperclip on her desk, 'sometime during the day you're going to have to speak to Ben — you know that, don't you?'

'I was hoping to stay out of his way as much as possible.'

'He's planning to hold the festival again next year and he needs your assistance. Do you have a problem with that?'

'Can we discuss this another time? Like that long winter's evening you were talking about?'

'Yes, yes, I'm coming.' Yvette inspected her pager with an impatient sigh. 'You'd better do your rounds, Fleur. Put yourself about. Let people see you're back. I nearly forgot — how's Abe?'

'On the mend. By the way, I bumped into James Day at the hospital. He's hoping to put in an appearance tomorrow.'

'James who?'

'The book tent manager. The new

father?' Fleur said, hoping to jog Yvette's memory.

'Better and better.' Yvette looked much happier than she had a few moments earlier. 'All right, I'm coming,' she shouted at her pager.

★   ★   ★

Snoozing grandparents and families indulging in much-needed refreshment breaks occupied the deckchairs dotted around the field. The main arena was a cacophony of noise as the swing band vied with the vintage puppet display, and the clowns' antics had everyone roaring with laughter. The public address system had given up trying to beat the competition, and volunteer students were busy circuiting the field, distributing leaflets detailing all the day's attractions.

'Here, pass them over.' Fleur earned herself a grateful smile as she offered to hand some of them out on her rounds.

Charlie Franconi's talk had proved poignant, heart-warming, and in places extremely funny. His tales of early circus life, the sacrifices he made, and his rise to stardom had entranced Fleur and his sell-out audience. The political memoirs she found heavy going, but they were well-patronised and provoked spirited discussions afterwards as the attendees descended on the refreshment tents.

Two children raced towards Fleur, flapping their questionnaires. 'Do you know where the battle of Ridgly Parva was fought?' one of them asked. 'We're trying to win first prize in the history quiz.'

'Go and ask that gentleman over there.' She indicated a tweed-suited professor. 'He knows all the answers.' With a whoop of glee, the youngsters raced off.

Phyllis teetered towards her on impossibly high heels. 'Darling, you're back.'

'So it would seem.'

She air kissed her daughter. 'Do mind my hat; it's a bit delicate. Now, what's all this nonsense about you and Ben having a falling-out?'

'Does everyone at the festival know my

personal business?' Fleur was beginning to lose patience.

'Just about.' Her mother's grey eyes twinkled back at her. 'But the Denmans are made of stern stuff. We can cope with a little local gossip, can't we?'

'If you say so.' Fleur didn't have the energy to enter into a spirited discussion with her mother.

'I'll let you in on a secret,' Phyllis confided. 'Two secrets, actually.'

'Should you be telling me if they're secret?'

'Yvette and Sandy, Rebecca and Piers.'

'What about them?'

Phyllis raised her eyebrows. 'I don't have to spell it out, do I?'

'Are you saying Yvette and Sandy ...' Fleur paused. 'What exactly *are* you saying?'

'It's official — they're an item. So are Rebecca and Piers.'

'No.' Fleur shook her head. 'Yvette's always been proud to lead the single life.'

'I think she's changed her mind.'

'With Sandy?'

'I know. I would have thought she'd have gone for one of the big hitters. Heaven knows there are enough of them around the place today. Do you know, I think I was wrong about Rebecca Ebony too. She's actually quite a nice person. We shared a taxi down from Castle Brampton this morning. That's when she told me she's got a thing going with Piers and that she and Ben are history.' Phyllis giggled like a young girl. 'Rather appropriate choice of words, 'history', don't you think?'

'What were you doing at Castle Brampton?'

A guilty expression crossed Phyllis's face. 'Goodness me, there's our local MP — I simply must go and introduce myself. Isn't he handsome? They say he's destined to go places.'

'If you're looking for Ben Salt,' said Jack Saunders, trotting by at a brisk pace, 'he's signing copies of his latest Rex Flint book. Lovely day, isn't it? Glad you didn't desert the cause.'

Fleur handed out a few more leaflets

before plucking up the courage to walk over to the book tent. If she were going to face Ben, perhaps it would be better to do so in full view.

Sandy relinquished his post by Ben's side. 'Exactly the person I want to see. I'm in need of a break. Can you get the queue into some sort of order and distribute the books? I've never known demand like it. I think the sun's gone to everyone's head.'

'To Sally please,' a young mother requested, handing over her copy of *Too Much Too Late* with an adoring smile. 'I love your books,' she gushed.

Ben signed the book with a flourish. Then as he handed it back, his eyes met Fleur's.

'Sandy's asked me to stand in for him,' she explained, determined not to flinch.

'Reinforcements,' the deputy manager said, depositing another pile of Ben's books on a side table. 'How's it going, folks?' Not waiting for their answer, he turned his attention back to the till. 'Gotta go. My public awaits.'

'Let's get out of here before he comes back with another pile.' Ben signed his last book and, grabbing Fleur's elbow, hustled her past a sea of inquisitive faces.

'I'd better go and see how things are on the re-enactment field,' she said.

'You're going nowhere until we've had a chance to catch up. I need a drink, and the only place we're going to get it in peace and quiet is up at the castle.'

'I promised Yvette I wouldn't leave unless I told three separate people where I was going,' Fleur protested. 'I don't think she trusts me not to disappear again.'

Ben muttered under his breath. 'Telling three people here that you and I are going off to the castle for a private drink would have the rumour machine going into overdrive.'

'I know a good place where you can get excellent leftovers. Follow me.'

'Where are we going?'

'Behind the VIP tent.'

⋆   ⋆   ⋆

'Hello again,' the friendly waitress greeted Fleur when they went inside. 'We've got more lovely nibbles today, but don't tell everyone or they'll all want a piece of the action.'

While she was talking, Ben sorted out two rickety garden seats. 'Who's going first?' he demanded after he'd dusted them down.

'I want to know what my mother was doing up the castle today,' said Fleur, 'and why she and Rebecca Ebony were sharing a taxi.'

'I'll swap you that for your version of exactly what happened yesterday afternoon. You wouldn't believe some of the stories I've heard.'

Rebecca rounded the corner, and for the third time that morning Fleur was caught up in a stranglehold. 'Fleur! I'm so glad you and Ben have made things up, because I have a teeny favour to ask of you both.'

'Not now,' Ben clipped back at her.

'Yes now,' Rebecca returned in an equally steely voice. 'It concerns sponsorship.'

'I'm done with guest appearances,' he told her.

'Good, because what I have in mind is hiding yourself away for another night in the hangar.'

'No way,' Ben said firmly.

'Piers and I have been invited to a sponsor's ball this evening. Ben, this is huge. If they agree to Phyllis's demands, you'll be able to hold the festival here for the next five years. Piers is being prickly because his machine is still spluttering. He's threatening to pull out of everything.' She rolled her eyes. 'And we've all been down that route, haven't we?'

'Becky,' Fleur said, reverting to Rebecca's school nickname, 'what have you done?'

'I've promised Piers that the two of you would clean out the last of his fuel system this evening.'

Her voice faded as she took in the expressions of horror on both their faces.

18

'What have I said? You both look as though I've announced a death in the family.'

'You've suggested I give up another night's sleep to work on Piers's biplane, and you're wondering why I'm not doing handsprings?' Ben cast her a look of disgust.

'I had no choice.' Rebecca looked at Fleur as if hoping for some support.

'How about suggesting someone else does the honours?' Ben enquired.

'You're the only person Piers trusts.' Rebecca flashed him her most winning smile.

'And you can stop smiling at me like that.' Ben looked in no mood for compromise. 'It won't work.'

Rebecca turned her attention to Fleur. 'How about you, Fleur? Wouldn't you welcome the chance to bond with

Ben? You've a lot of things to get through.'

'Such as?' It was Fleur's turn to play tough cop.

'Well …' Rebecca gave a nervous laugh. 'This business of next year's festival, for a start.'

'Nothing has been decided,' Ben intervened.

'Exactly. You need to get down to it.'

With a sinking heart, Fleur recognised the expression on Rebecca's face. She was out to make mischief.

'Then, of course,' Rebecca said slowly and clearly, 'there's the other issue.'

'What other issue?' Fleur asked.

'Surely you don't need me to spell it out.'

'I think I do.'

'Phyllis has done her bit,' Rebecca began, avoiding a direct answer, 'so the rest is up to you.' She made a gesture with her hands suggesting a fait accompli. 'I'm not saying any more.'

'On the whole,' Fleur said, avoiding looking at Ben, 'I preferred you when you were Becky the Bully.'

'Whatever can you mean?' Rebecca widened her falsely innocent eyes.

'At least we knew where we stood.'

'You mean you can't cope with the new me?'

'Yes, I do mean that.'

'Well, it's something you're going to have to get used to. Blame Piers.'

'For what?' Ben was looking more confused than ever.

'You know,' Rebecca confided, 'this place is better than an internet dating site. Yvette's fallen for Sandy. Then Piers and I ... well, who would have thought it? He's a grease monkey and I hate things in fields, but the chemistry's there. Piers is going to teach me how to fly, and then I think I might go on a mechanics course.'

Ben made such a disbelieving noise at the back of his throat that both Fleur and Rebecca cast him a disgusted look.

'What's wrong with you?' Rebecca demanded.

He did his best to maintain a composed expression. 'The name Rebecca

Ebony and mechanics courses really don't belong in the same sentence.'

'If you're going to take that attitude,' she shot back — and there was a trace of the old Rebecca as she tossed her head, 'then we have nothing else to say.'

'Rebecca Ebony to the book tent immediately. Rebecca Ebony, please,' the tannoy stuttered.

'I expect supplies of my new book have arrived.' Rebecca was all smiles again. 'I'll save you a copy, Fleur. Don't let me down, Ben.'

'She's right, you know.' Ben stood up.

'About what?' Fleur's legs wobbled as she followed his example.

'We can't talk now. See you tonight, ten o'clock. Wear something warm and bring a flask of hot coffee and sandwiches.'

Before Fleur could protest, Ben had gone.

★　★　★

Silver moonlight cast ghostly images on the deserted field, and a soft breeze disturbed the mechanism of the galloper, creating an eerie whine. An owl swooped over Castle Brampton, silhouetted on the top of the hill. Fleur shivered with a sense of unease. The scene was like something out of a late-night movie. Strange shapes loomed at her out of the darkness, and she was seriously tempted to abandon Ben to his fate. She had toyed with the idea of not turning up but realised that would be the coward's way out. She owed Ben an explanation for her reluctance to commit to next year's festival.

'Who's there?' A torch flashed.

'It's me,' she replied.

'Fleur?' Jack Saunders queried. 'Don't you ever go home?'

'Ben's working on the biplane,' she explained.

'And you've come to join him? There's nothing like a bit of moonlight to create a romantic atmosphere. I'll make sure you're not disturbed. There's a heater in the security hut if you get cold. See you tomorrow.' He saluted and sauntered away.

Fleur stood where she was for a few moments. Why was everyone trying to get involved in her nonexistent love life? Hadn't Ben proved exactly how he felt about her when Rebecca accused her of making off with the book tent takings? Her past would always create a shadow between them, and it would never go away.

'Fleur? Over here,' another voice called out. She spun round. A figure waved at her. 'In the old barn.'

Ben was dressed in a boiler suit and a knitted woolly hat. 'Is that coffee? I could do with something to warm me up. My hands are stiff and my toes have gone numb.'

'Jack said we could use the heater in the security hut,' Fleur said.

'Then let's get on over.'

The hut was deserted but warm. Ben sat on one of the canvas chairs while Fleur poured out two steaming mugs of coffee. 'Are you hungry?' she asked.

'The only food I've had all day was those salmon canapé things, and they weren't very filling.' He wolfed down two cheese and tomato doorstep sandwiches. 'Aren't you having any?'

'Maybe later.'

Fleur's stomach was in knots. Ben had removed his woolly hat, and the static reduced his hair to a spiky mess. Fleur fought down the urge to flatten it.

'This reminds me of the time Sandy and I were stuck in the desert.' He finished his sandwich and wiped an oily hand down the side of his boiler suit.

'Does it?' Fleur transferred her attention back to what he was saying.

'We were lost. The sun had gone down and we didn't have a clue where we were. We thought we were going to die of cold; then some cowboys rescued us. They built a fire and boiled water and shared their tucker. Were we pleased to see them.'

'What were they doing in the desert?'

'They said they were extras in a film being shot further down the valley, and that the director was looking for a stunt man.' Ben smiled at the memory. 'The rest is history.'

In the warmth of the hut, Fleur relaxed and sipped her coffee. 'Do you miss the life?' she asked.

'Occasionally, but it was time to come home. I love riding my bike but my bones were beginning to protest. Some days I fell off more than a dozen times, and there's only so much of that treatment a body can take.'

'Why did you choose Ridgly Parva?'

'My mother used to holiday here as a child. She always spoke of the area with such fondness; and when I discovered Castle Brampton was up for sale, I went for it. It seemed like the right thing to do.'

'And Sandy?'

'What about him?'

'Will he set up home here?'

'His main home is in France. When all this is over —' Ben gestured towards the festival field. '— I expect he'll want to go back.'

'And you?' Fleur didn't know why she was asking so many questions, but it seemed important to learn as much about Ben as she could.

'I'm staying. I'm already working on my next Rex Flint.' He poured out some more coffee. 'Now it's your turn. Tell me about you and Yvette.'

'We went to school together: Yvette, Rebecca — Becky, as she was called in those days — and me.' Fleur paused. 'After I left, Yvette was the only one who stayed in touch.'

'It must have been tough for you,' Ben sympathised.

'It was a difficult time for the whole family.'

'How did you and Yvette get together for this gig?'

'When the Ridgly Parva festival was first talked about, Yvette asked if I'd be interested in acting as liaison officer. I jumped at the chance. It isn't easy getting work when you've got a background like mine, but I'm sure I'm not telling you something you don't already know.' Her eyes flashed a challenge at Ben.

'Your mother told me how difficult things were.'

'Could we change the subject please?'

Her voice wavered.

Ben looked at her intently. 'I'm on your side,' he said.

'You make it sound like war.' Fleur attempted a smile.

'Sometimes every day is a battle, but you just have to get on with it.'

A silence fell between them. In the corner of the hut, the two-bar heater glowed red. Fleur stared at it, unable to think of anything to say.

'Did you know the idea for my motorbike was originally thought up by two aircraft pilots?' Ben changed the subject.

Fleur swallowed some more of her coffee. 'I have to admit I didn't.'

'Piers told me. He's a petrol-head as well as a flying ace. He likes all things mechanical.'

'He's been a big draw for the festival.'

'That's why I wanted to help him out tonight. I owe him several favours.'

'Shouldn't we be getting back?' Fleur suggested.

'I've nearly finished — are you listening?' Ben prompted as Fleur's eyes strayed to the window behind him.

'There's someone snooping around outside.' Fleur's voice was a faint whisper.

Ben crossed the room in two strides and yanked open the door. A security guard tumbled in.

'Sorry,' he apologised. 'I could hear voices and I thought maybe the action group had been resurrected and was planning more trouble. I wasn't spying on you.'

'And we've outstayed our welcome here,' Ben said. 'You can have your hut back.'

'You don't have to go on my account.'

'We'll be in the barn with the biplane, so if you'd put the word round, we shouldn't cause any more security scares.'

'Will do.' The security guard settled down in the chair vacated by Ben and picked up a copy of the festival newsletter. 'I see Abe Groves did himself a nasty yesterday. What did he think he was playing at? Glad you sorted him out, Fleur.'

She flushed under the stark lighting of

the security hut, aware that Ben's eyes were fixed on her.

'Thanks for your hospitality,' she said to the guard. 'We'd best be going.'

'Hold the lantern steady.'

They went back to the barn, and Ben bent over the biplane cockpit.

'Do you think it'll fly tomorrow?' Fleur asked.

'Like a bird. It'll be a much bigger attraction than my bike.' His voice was muffled. 'There we are.' He stood up straight. 'All done.'

'Aren't you going to test it?'

'I'll leave it to Piers to do tomorrow. He'll be here bright and early. He always is.'

'Then I think I'd better be getting home,' Fleur said, relieved she wasn't going to have to spend the entire night in Ben's company.

'We can talk here if you like, but it'll be much more comfortable up at the castle.'

A fox screeched in the far field. 'Vixens always make that noise,' Ben assured a jumpy Fleur.

'I know, but I don't think I'll ever get used to it.'

He drew her body close against his. 'You're quite safe with me,' he assured her. 'Now, about our talk.'

'What do you want to talk about?'

'Us,' he said, and drawing her body against his, he kissed her.

19

Sandy was in the kitchen, tucking into cheese on toast. 'Don't mind me. I'll be out of your way in a minute, so there's no need to glower, Ben.'

'I thought you'd gone out to dinner with Yvette.'

Sandy pulled a face. 'So did I, but Piers insisted she go to the ball with him and Rebecca.'

'Weren't you invited?' Fleur asked.

Sandy shuddered. 'Not my sort of thing at all. I always want to pass judgment on the wine.'

'You're such a snob,' Ben retaliated.

'It's my business. Besides, I've got loads of my own work to catch up on,' Sandy said, refusing to rise to the bait. 'I'm hosting a seminar at the château the week after next. Yvette's helping with the public relations. There's always lots to do beforehand.' He pushed away his plate.

'Kitchen's all yours. Don't keep him up too late, Fleur; we've got a busy day tomorrow.' He kissed her on the cheek; then, snatching a banana out of the fruit bowl, he made his way upstairs.

Fleur looked expectantly at Ben.

'Coffee?' he queried.

She shook her head.

'Good decision. We're both awash with the stuff.' He poured out a glass of water and sat down.

Fleur pulled out a kitchen chair and joined him, ignoring the triple beat of her heart. She knew she should have resisted his embrace, but after all she had been through she lacked the willpower. The feel of his arms around her body had transported her to a place of comfort and safety. She clenched her fists. She had to stay focused. Life wasn't a fairytale. She mustn't let Ben persuade her to change her mind.

'With Yvette in France, you could be out of a job next week,' he said.

'It's the nature of my work. My contract was only for the Ridgly Parva festival.'

'I can offer you a job.'

'I've already explained my position.'

'You're scared to face up to the past?'

'That's a ridiculous assumption.'

'Is it? Ridgly Parva has got over what happened. Now it's your turn.'

'You don't understand.'

'I understand very well,' Ben countered.

'Did your father get the blame for something he didn't do?'

'No,' he admitted.

'Then how can you possibly know what it's like if you haven't been in that situation?'

'I didn't even know my father. My mother worked hard to give my sister and me a good education, and like Phyllis she was very proud of her children. If nothing else, you owe it to Phyllis to move on with your life.'

'I have.'

'Then accept my offer.'

'There may not be a history festival next year.'

'I'm not talking about the festival.'

'Then what are you talking about?'

'Rex Flint.'

Fleur picked up Ben's glass of water and took a gulp. 'What has Rex Flint got to do with us?'

'There's talk about his books being made into a television series, and I need some help.'

'I know nothing about television production.'

'Neither do I,' Ben said, 'but with Sandy going off to France and taking Yvette with him, I need someone I can trust to look after my affairs.'

'You're asking me to be your agent?'

'I was hoping to combine it with a deeper relationship.'

'Do you mind if I open a window?' Fleur asked.

Ben unwound his long legs from under the table and, crossing the kitchen, let in some night air. 'Is that better?'

'Thank you.'

He sat down again. 'From the moment I first saw you covered in mud, ready to do battle with me, I wanted to be a part of your life, Fleur — but you pushed me away every time I tried to get close to you. I thought at first it was because of Rebecca. Then you were so prickly about your past.'

'Is it any wonder?'

'No one really believed you were responsible for the disappearance of the book tent money.'

'You did.'

'I never accused you of anything.'

'Yes you did. You accused me of flooding your wretched kitchen, remember?'

A look of regret crossed Ben's face. 'Sandy has a lot to answer for, but we're straying off the point.'

'What *was* the point, exactly?'

'I did suspect Rebecca of stirring things up, and I think the situation would probably have continued if Piers hadn't created a useful distraction. With other things on her mind, her vendetta against you died away.'

'Why?'

'Why what?' Ben looked puzzled.

'Why would Rebecca try to close down

the festival?'

'She didn't. Things got out of hand. She wanted the festival to be a success, but I suspect she was jealous of you.'

'That doesn't make sense.'

'It's the way her mind works. She saw how I felt about you and she acted accordingly.'

'You have a high opinion of yourself.' Fleur was seething. 'And if you think your feelings for me are reciprocated, then you're wrong.'

'You'd better let me have that,' Ben said quietly, easing the tumbler out of her hands, 'before you break the glass.'

The touch of his fingers on hers was as sharp as an electric shock. Fleur bit her lip in an effort not to flinch.

'Is it Abe Groves?' Ben asked.

Fleur frowned. 'Abe?'

'What exactly is the relationship between you?'

'Abe and his family stood by us when people crossed the road rather than speak to my mother or me. Don't you dare start saying unkind things about him.'

'That's what I mean.'

'Say again?'

'You're always ready to leap to his defence, and I wondered if you and he were more than old friends.'

'We are. But despite rumours to the contrary, I have no intention of eloping with Abe — and if I did, I'd make sure the car we used was full of petrol.' Fleur ran out of breath. 'Does that answer your question?'

'This is getting us nowhere.' Ben ran a hand through his hair.

'You were the one who invited me up here to talk,' Fleur reminded him.

'You're right. It's time to get down to business.' He looked expectantly at her. 'Do you want time to think about my proposal?'

'I've already given you my answer.'

'It's tiring work proposing, and I've never done it before. I didn't make a very good job of it, did I?'

Fleur stared at Ben in bewilderment. 'What exactly are you proposing?'

'It was my intention to ask you to

marry me, but as usual Sandy got in the way of things, and then you've been looking at me so weirdly that I've lost my nerve.'

'I thought you wanted me to be your agent.'

'And you turned me down. So how about my second offer?'

'My answer is no to both offers.'

'If you don't accept, he'll only go on asking you until you do,' said Sandy, who was lounging in the doorway. 'That's how I was conned into being his agent.' He smiled at Fleur. 'And don't worry — I won't be upset if you take my place. I was never a very good agent anyway. My heart wasn't in it.'

Ben spun round at the sound of his voice. 'I thought you were catching up on your backlog.'

'The washing machine's packed up again.'

'You'll have to sort it out yourself,' Ben snapped. 'And stop eavesdropping on a private conversation.'

'I wasn't, but I could hear every word

you were saying in the laundry,' Sandy complained.

'Before the two of you come to blows,' Fleur jumped in, seizing the initiative, 'it's time I went home.'

Sandy took another piece of fruit out of the bowl. 'It's a long walk.'

'I'll call a taxi.'

'Ben could give you a lift.' He bit into his apple. 'Though it's very cold on the back of his motorbike at this time of night — and I speak from experience.'

'He won't need to give you a lift, Fleur,' came a woman's voice. 'Our taxi is still outside.'

Sandy hastily swallowed a mouthful of apple. 'Rebecca,' he greeted the new arrival. 'How was the ball?'

Piers, standing behind her, undid his black tie. 'I hate wearing these things,' he admitted, 'but I've got you lots of useful contacts, Sandy.'

Sandy's face lit up. 'You're a star.' He began to usher Piers out of the kitchen. 'We'll talk about it in the lounge. Fleur, don't let Ben bully you into doing anything you don't want to do.'

Rebecca was the first to speak after Sandy had hustled Piers away. 'Have I interrupted something?'

'Ben and I have said all we've got to say,' Fleur replied.

'It would seem we have,' Ben said, acknowledging her words with a nod of his head.

'Well if you're ready to leave, Fleur, then so am I,' said Rebecca. 'Night, Ben. See you tomorrow.'

★   ★   ★

'Piers had had enough,' Rebecca confided to Fleur as their taxi drew away from Castle Brampton, 'so we left early. Funny, isn't it? I used to love those sorts of occasions, but now all I want to do is be with Piers.'

'Where's Yvette?' Fleur asked.

'She left early too, but Phyllis was still going strong.' Rebecca smiled. 'She's quite some lady, isn't she? You're so lucky to have her as a mother.'

'I know,' Fleur replied.

Rebecca cast her a sideways glance. 'Just to set the record straight, there never was anything between me and Ben. I suppose I was pressing all the wrong buttons, but I couldn't see it at the time. That's why I was such a nuisance to you. Am I forgiven?'

'It's time to draw a curtain over the past,' Fleur agreed.

'I think so too, but I don't suppose I'll ever forget the time you hacked off half my hair or when Yvette tied my laces together. Still,' Rebecca acknowledged with a quirky smile, 'one must move on. Now I have Piers and you have Ben.'

'No I don't,' Fleur contradicted her.

'Ben's one of the good guys,' Rebecca insisted. 'Can't you see that?'

'I wish everyone would stop interfering.'

'It's because we want the best for you, Fleur. You were badly treated in the past and we're doing our best to make up for it. Don't turn us away.'

Unused to such kindness from her old

adversary, Fleur blinked at Rebecca in the darkness of the cab.

'Friends?' Rebecca held up her hand.

'Friends.'

They slapped palms as the taxi began to slow down.

'See you tomorrow?' Rebecca said.

Fleur saw her waving through the back window as the taxi's tail-lights disappeared into the darkness.

★   ★   ★

'Thank you, everybody, for making the festival such a success.'

Clapping and cheering threatened to drown Phyllis's speech.

'Now for the good news. I have been reliably informed that Ridgly Parva will be hosting another festival next year on Brampton's Field, so if the mud hasn't put you off I hope you'll all be back. We've had a few hiccups along the way, but we came out triumphant in the end. I have to thank everyone for their hard work. Same time next year?'

Loud applause greeted her words.

'Now,' Phyllis continued, adjusting her bright orange picture hat that had become dislodged from the enthusiasm with which she had delivered her closing speech, 'James Day, new father and bookseller extraordinaire, has something to say.'

Clutching a small pink bundle from which a tiny tuft of hair was protruding, a smiling James walked onto the stage. 'I wanted to introduce everyone to my new baby daughter, Isla,' he announced. Then, lowering his voice, he said, 'And I'd be grateful if you'd keep the noise down. We've only just got her to sleep.'

The applause was instantly quelled.

'The other reason I'm here is to publicly apologise to Fleur Denman, who I believe, through no fault of her own, got the blame for the missing book tent takings. On behalf of Sandy and myself, and not forgetting Isla — sorry, Fleur.'

Fleur had been doing her best to maintain a low profile at the side of the stage, but now with all eyes on her she had no choice but to accept James's invitation to join him on the stage.

Carrying a huge bouquet of red roses, Amanda tiptoed across the stage and presented them to Fleur. 'The Day family would like to say thank you for everything,' she announced. 'I know we've got to keep our voices down, but I have one more request.'

A hush fell on the expectant crowd as Amanda stage-whispered into the microphone.

'We hope you'll do us the honour of being godmother to baby Isla.'

James had joined his wife and was now also smiling at Fleur. 'We're not taking no for an answer, are we?' He said, looking to the crowd for support. A sea of programmes was waved back at him. 'I've heard a rumour you're thinking of leaving us. Is it true?'

'I've made no plans.' Fleur did her best to keep her voice steady as she spoke through her bouquet of roses.

'Everyone wants you to stay,' James insisted, 'including Isla.' Right on cue,

Isla let out a loud wail. 'See? Even my daughter agrees with me, and you can't let your goddaughter down.'

Fleur was forced to shake her head. 'No, I can't,' she whispered.

'So, what's it to be?'

'I'd be honoured to be Isla's godmother.'

'Good. That's settled, then.' James waved to the crowd. 'See you all next year.'

Everyone began to drift away in the direction of the barbecue, leaving Fleur alone on the stage struggling with her emotions. Ridgly Parva had held out the hand of friendship. Rebecca had told her everyone was doing their best to make things up to her. Perhaps it was time to move on from the past.

Behind Fleur the boarding creaked. She turned to face Ben.

20

She had been careful to avoid his company all day, but there was no getting away from him now. They were alone on the deserted stage. The lights were dimmed, and the dying sun cast golden shadows on Ben's tousled hair. From the dark circles under his eyes, Fleur suspected he too had spent a sleepless night.

'We can't talk here.' His voice was husky and caught in his throat.

'Do we need to?' Her own voice was far from steady.

Since her early-morning talk with Phyllis — when her mother had told her in no uncertain terms that Ben was the man for her, and what was she thinking of playing around with his affections? — Fleur had come to terms with the inevitable. She had fought against her feelings from the beginning, but she could deny them no longer. She was in love with Ben

Salt, a man she had known for only seven days.

'This way,' he said.

Fleur raised no protest as Ben put out a hand to guide her down the rickety backstage steps.

'Watch your footing.' He flattened a clump of grass with the heel of his boot. Fleur, still clutching her roses, followed on behind.

'Where are we going?' She cast an anxious glance over her shoulder, fearing their progress might be attracting attention.

'You'll see.' Ben betrayed no such inhibitions, waving to a group of stragglers makings its way towards the marquee hosting the farewell gig.

'Not joining us?' one of them asked.

'Catch up with you later. Fleur and I have some unfinished business,' he called back.

'What did you have to say that for?' She winced as she collided with the decorative studs on the back of Ben's biker jacket. A shower of rose petals floated to the ground.

He looked at her. 'It's true, isn't it?'

'Yes, but we don't want everyone at the festival putting their own interpretation on our situation.'

'They've done that already,' Ben said in an infuriatingly calm voice. 'And here we are,' he announced.

'The admin tent?' Fleur wrinkled her nose as more rose petals tickled her face.

'I should imagine it's the one place on site that'll be deserted now the business of the day is over.'

In the background, the Hayseeds began to strike up a medley of old favourites. Fleur deposited her roses on an abandoned schedule that had been tossed across Yvette's desk. The damp stems stained the discarded notes. Fleur dabbed at them with a tissue but with little success.

'I don't suppose it matters now,' she muttered, and replaced her tissue in her pocket. She glanced up at Ben, who was positioned in front of the safe with his arms crossed, and waited for him to speak.

'At this moment nothing matters except us,' he said.

'Why did you bring me here?' Fleur demanded.

'I've never been a quitter, and we have some unfinished business.'

'Do we?'

'Can't you guess what it is?'

Fleur wasn't finding it easy to look Ben in the eye. 'We've said everything there is to say between us — several times.'

'That's what I mean about me not being a quitter. I don't give up easy. I want you to stay.'

'I've told you my reasons why that's not possible.' Fleur shook her head.

'And I don't believe a word of them.'

Fleur was finding it impossible to think straight as Ben moved in closer. She fiddled with a stray petal, which he removed from her fingers and flicked into the waste-paper bin.

'Are you saying I'm not telling the truth?' Fleur challenged.

'I'm saying you're looking for reasons to turn me down, and I want you to tell me why.'

'I can't.' Her voice was as husky as his.

'Why not?' he asked.

She shook her head.

'I was right, wasn't I? It's because your heart isn't in them?'

Fleur was running out of things to say. Everything Ben said was true, but how could she commit?

'Is it because like me, you can't believe what's happened between us?'

Fleur raised her eyes to Ben's. 'Nothing's happened between us.'

'There you go again,' Ben sighed. 'Denying the obvious. It's not good enough. If nothing else, you owe me a proper explanation.'

Fleur hesitated before speaking. 'You mentioned not knowing your father.'

'He died when I was a baby, as did your parents.'

'You know what happened?'

'Phyllis told me.'

'I wasn't a baby. I was young enough to remember my parents, and the transition wasn't easy. At that stage of my life I wasn't a very nice person.'

'I don't need to know any of that,' Ben said in a quiet voice.

'I can't help feeling it was my fault my father got involved in the organic farming project.'

'Why?'

'He always wanted the best for me. I think it was to compensate for my unhappy childhood.'

'Life happens. Your father made a decision. It was the wrong one, but it wasn't your fault.'

'Not everyone saw it like that.'

'To blazes with everyone else.' An angry frown creased Ben's forehead.

'What if the same thing happens to you?'

'Say again?'

'The festival eats up money. Suppose things don't work out.'

'That is not going to happen. The festival has more than covered its expenses. And even if it hadn't, the Rex Flint novels could sub them. So, any more excuses?'

An explosion in the background made

Fleur jump. She looked past Ben to where the sky was streaked with vermilion and green stars.

'They could have chosen a better time to let off their rockets.' Ben's eyes were still fixed on Fleur's face.

'Aren't they pretty?' A smile softened the expression in her eyes as a shower of golden studs lit up the night sky.

'Don't use shootings stars as an excuse not to answer my question.'

'Do you really want me to stay on?' she asked.

'How many times do I have to repeat myself?'

'You don't mind about my past?'

'It's the future that interests me — ours — and I want us to spend it together.'

'And Sandy?'

'He can look after himself. Besides, he'll have Yvette to keep him on track.'

'I suppose if Yvette can change her mind about a long-term relationship ...' Fleur began.

'She has. She and Sandy are getting it together. So that only leaves you and me.'

'Put like that, how can I refuse?'

'You're staying on?'

'Didn't I just say that?'

Ben hesitated. 'I'm not sure. I've got it wrong so many times this past week, would you mind repeating yourself?' He was forced to raise his voice against a cacophony of exploding rockets.

'Why? Have you got a recording device hidden away in the pockets of your leather jacket?'

Ben held up his arms. 'Why don't you search me?'

Fleur flushed and turned her head away. 'That won't be necessary.'

'I want to make sure I hear every word you say,' he said in her ear. She could feel him breathing down her neck.

'I want to stay on,' Fleur repeated slowly and carefully. 'Was that clear enough for you?'

'What made you change your mind?'

'I ran out of arguments,' she admitted.

'At last we agree on something.' Ben was backing her against the canvas flaps of the tent. 'In order to save any more confusion, what do you want to stay on as — my gopher?' Fleur frowned in confusion. 'Someone who goes for this and goes for that,' Ben enlightened her.

'Is there another option? I'm sort of maxed out on being a gopher.'

'There is,' Ben conceded, 'but it's one I'm reluctant to suggest.'

'Why?'

'You've already turned it down twice.'

'I thought you weren't a quitter,' Fleur taunted him.

'In that case,' Ben said, moving even closer, 'we've established that you don't want to be my gopher.'

'We have,' Fleur agreed.

'Then would you settle for being my wife?'

'How can you fall in love in the space of a week?'

'That's not an answer.'

'I would answer yes, but ...' Fleur paused.

'Now what?' Ben heaved a sigh.

'It'd mean you having the mayor as a mother-in-law.'

'That is a serious set back,' he admitted. 'But I think I can cope with it.'

'As well as the mother-of-the-bride hat?'

'Perhaps you could have a quiet word in her ear.'

'I could try, but I don't think I'll have much success.'

Ben nodded. 'She's bound to make the headlines isn't she?'

'I'm afraid so.'

'Why don't we cross that bridge when we come to it?'

'Agreed.'

'Now for the last time, will you marry me?'

'I will,' Fleur agreed, before Ben's lips descended on hers.

We do hope that you have enjoyed reading this large print book.

Did you know that all of our titles are available for purchase?

We publish a wide range of high quality large print books including:
Romances, Mysteries, Classics
General Fiction
Non Fiction and Westerns

Special interest titles available in large print are:
The Little Oxford Dictionary
Music Book, Song Book
Hymn Book, Service Book

Also available from us courtesy of Oxford University Press:
Young Readers' Dictionary
(large print edition)
Young Readers' Thesaurus
(large print edition)

For further information or a free brochure, please contact us at:
Ulverscroft Large Print Books Ltd.,
The Green, Bradgate Road, Anstey,
Leicester, LE7 7FU, England.
Tel: (00 44) **0116 236 4325**
Fax: (00 44) **0116 234 0205**